CHRISTMAS AT CEDARWOOD CABIN

JADE WILKES

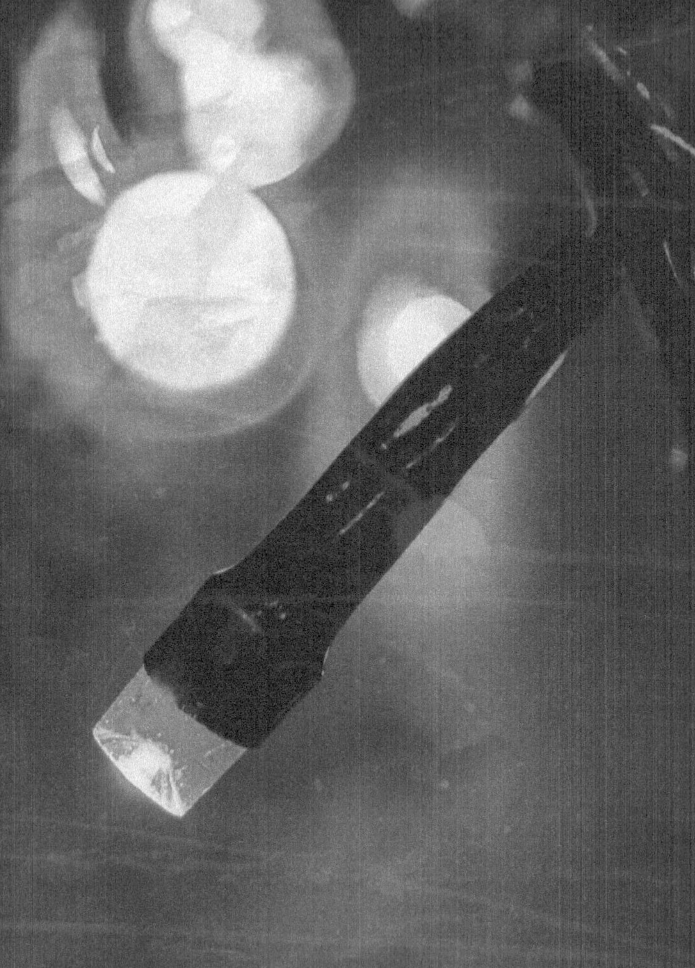

Editing: Alexa at The Fiction Fix
Formatting & Cover Design: Disturbed Valkyrie Designs
Emotional Support Gamers: Callum, Maddie & Cat

CHRISTMAS AT CEDARWOOD CABIN

This is a continuation of *Cedarwood Cabin*. I highly recommend reading that book first in order to grasp the story fully.

Happy Xmas (War Is Over) - John Lennon
Shake Up Christmas - Train
Santa Baby - Kylie Minogue
Left Outside Alone - Anastacia
Power of Love - Frankie Goes To Hollywood
Too Lost in You - Sugababes

ONE

FLORA

I step out onto the balcony, feeling the usual creak of the wood beneath my feet. It's freezing, the air nipping at my cheeks, but my coffee mug warms me, the steam rising in delicate little spirals, only to disappear into the wintery air. The forest that stretches out in front of me is so breathtakingly beautiful, it should be on a Christmas card. Thick, fresh snow has settled on the ground, not a single human footprint anywhere. I take a deep breath, and for a second, I forget about everything else. The snow glitters in the faint morning sun, each flake reflecting the light of its rays. Beyond the trees, I spy bear prints in the snow. Before sunrise, they must have made a beeline for the garbage cans beside the cabin. I can't help but shake my head. *Damn bears.*

There they go again, rummaging through the trash no matter how hard we try to keep them away. It's the little things that remind me of the wild nature all around us.

This Christmas feels different—like, really different. It's my first one without my dad, and that hits me like a ton of bricks. He loved Christmas. He'd have been the first one out here on the balcony, totally amazed by the snow, insistent on making snow angels and taking pictures to remember it all. But now, it's just me and them: Dax and Lyka. My men, as I like to call them. I smile at the thought as I take another sip of my coffee. They are my everything. With them, the part of me that was so hollow for so long finally feels full. They are my family, my sanctuary.

Honestly, I can't imagine my life without them. We've had our ups and downs, and some days were tough. When the winter hit, I was left wondering if I called the right shots. But isn't that life? Even through the bad days, they've been there, keeping me level-headed and giving me something to smile about.

The cabin door opens with a creak, bringing me back to reality. I don't even need to look; I know who it is–Lyka. He has this vibe to the way he moves, and it totally gives him away. Before any words can escape my lips, his arms come around my shoulders from behind, strong and warm, pulling me into his chest.

"How's my girl this morning?" he whispers, nudging my ear with his lips. That voice of his makes my knees weak every single time. I lean into him, savoring his warmth.

I tilt my head to the side, and he plants a quick kiss on my cheek. "I'm good. Just soaking in the view."

"It's beautiful, isn't it?" he says, tightening his hold.

"Mhmm."

"I mean, it's not as beautiful as you."

I laugh; I can't help myself. That's his charm–making ordinary moments special. Swaying a bit in his arms, I look up at him. When our eyes meet, his sparkle.

"You sound so cheesy right now," I reply, rolling my eyes. *To think, this man used to be grumpy with me.*

Lyka grabs my chin. "Don't make me put you on the naughty list this Christmas."

He looks at me with a familiar possessiveness, the same

kind he carried when they lied about a lockdown, but his serious face soon twists into a beautiful, goofy grin. *Fuck, that jawline.*

He leans in to press light kisses against my neck.

The naughty list? I wonder if that means being tied up in the barn with tinsel around my throat.

I shake off the thought. "Is Dax out of the shower yet?"

Lyka's attitude changes immediately. He steps back, leaving a gap between us. "I don't know."

I let out a sigh and glance at the cabin door. These last few weeks, Dax has been quiet, more withdrawn. He's here physically—but mentally, he's somewhere else. When I try to ask, to understand what's wrong, he cuts me off mid-question, his responses blunt.

"Lyka," I try to sound firm, "tell me what's up with him. Is it me?"

Lyka stares at me for a moment before his eyes flicker to the trees, like he's looking for an escape route. "It's not you. All I can say is, this time of year is rough on him."

Irritation and worry well up inside me, and I bite the inside of my cheek. Trying to read between the lines, I scan his face. "Did your—" I choke. "Did your parents die around this time?"

Lyka shakes his head. "Look, it's not really my place to say. It's up to him to fill you in. I'm sorry, Flora." He inches closer, his hand reaching to gently stroke my cheek. "He'll talk to you when he is ready. Don't push him. Come on, let's get inside. It's freezing."

I glance back at the forest one last time and then nod, letting Lyka guide me to the door. In reality, my mind is miles away from the cold, thinking about Dax, praying that when he finally opens up, I'm there to help him.

TWO

DAX

I sit cross-legged on the rug by the fire in my room as the wood crackles. The dancing flames consuming everything in their path are mesmerizing; I can't look away. How can something so dangerous be so pleasing? So damn beautiful? My jaw clenches as that thought continues to circle in my mind. It's kind of perfect. The fire could be a mirror reflecting me and Lyka: on the surface, we're loyal, charismatic, handsome. But beneath that? Beneath lies destruction, pain, and regret.

Flora doesn't see it, or maybe she doesn't want to. She looks at us as though we're her personal heaven. If only she knew the blood covering my hands or saw the shadows playing in my head this time of year. I feel my chest tighten; the air in the room suddenly vanishes.

I hate this time of year, that damn Christmas song, the blood.

I bring my knees to my chest and embrace them tightly, as if that could hold everything inside. I rock back and forth, barely conscious of the movement. What did I do? The memories peck at my brain, relentless, sharp.

My hands shake as I run my fingers through my hair, pulling at the roots in frustration. Flora knows I've been acting different. She's not dumb. I can see the way she looks at me, all soft-eyed yet still inquiring, searching for answers I just can't bring myself to give. I want to tell her, I do, but how can I? What if she wants to leave after I tell her?

I held her hostage and forced her to stay when she had no choice. I vowed I'd never do that again, never push her to do anything, never make her feel trapped.

What if she looks at me like he did?

It cuts through my brain like a hot knife. I can remember my adoptive dad standing there, staring, his eyes bulged in shock and fear when he saw the bodies.

My little sister. She was mine.

I don't want Flora to see this side of me. She has seen enough—far too much, really. The very thought of her finding out what I'm capable of is unbearable. She is the only thing in this existence that makes it at all worth it. Losing her is simply not an option.

I'll chain her up again. No! Fuck! What am I thinking?

My fists clench, and I pound them against my head to push those images away, to shut up some of the voices that won't fuck off. With each strike, his voice—*the devil's voice*—gets a little louder, yelling at me, mocking me.

I don't hear the door open, nor do I hear Lyka's footsteps until he's there. His hands clamp on my wrists and jerk them away. The sudden movement sends me crashing to the wood floor.

"Dax! Stop. Seriously, just stop!" Lyka's voice cuts through the air. He has me pinned down, his weight crushing me into the cold floor, and I can't help but let out a ragged, painful sob.

"Shh, I've got you," he says, hauling me up and squeezing me in a tight hug.

I don't fight it. That wall I built up breaks. I press my face into his chest, crying hard, shaking against him.

"Where's Flora?" I sob. Just thinking about her walking in, seeing me like this, weak and broken... It's too much.

"She's in the shower. It's all right, she's fine," Lyka reassures me.

The room falls silent save for my sobs, and then I catch it: an airy melody wafting through the silence. Flora's voice emanates from the bathroom as she sings some tune. She sounds so vivacious, her voice driving back the darkness, like sunshine bursting through thick forest. I let my eyes close for a moment.

"Dax, I can never forgive my folks," Lyka says, still clinging to me. "They shouldn't have let you go back to your parents. I should have stopped them."

I can feel the years of anger and regret in what he says.

"No, no!" My voice breaks as I lean back to look him in the eye. "I found them, Lyka. I decided to go back. Don't put this on your parents. I killed your father." A tear falls down my cheek. "He started drinking because of me and what he had to cover up."

Lyka's face tightens, and his jaw clenches as he stares at me. "No! He started drinking after my mother's death. You know that... That's what we tell people," he says, his voice rising. "Dax, you were scared. You did what you had to do. You were a confused kid who didn't know any better."

I can't bear his stare any longer. Memories refuse to let me go, and I am too tired to push them back.

"Dax, it wasn't on you what they did. You hear me? It was never ever your fault. Your parents were fucked up people, and they took all that crap out on you and your sister. My parents shouldn't have let you go back."

I really want to believe him, I do. "I killed them," I mutter, the words escaping before I can catch myself. "I went back, and I killed them, Lyka. Does that sound like something a victim does?"

"A victim does that to survive. You lived through two weeks of hell. That devil did unthinkable things to you and your sister. There's a part of me that feels guilty."

Lyka and I hold each other like we haven't in ages, not since we were kids. It almost feels new between us, but this is what I need. I can't blame my adoptive parents for letting me go back to my birth parents. I mean, how were they to know? *I* tracked them down. *I* wanted to find out where I came from. I thought I would find some answers, but instead, I dropped myself into hell.

Two weeks, just fourteen days, yet those two weeks felt like forever. My little sister endured it for years before I arrived. Then, we endured the beating, yelling, and sickening games together. The devil was nonstop, and his wife, my so-called mom, stood there and did nothing. She watched, her face cold and distant, like we were objects, things to be used and tossed aside.

I tried hard to protect my little sister. She was just a kid, small and fragile. Every time I tried to intervene, he took all his anger out on me instead. That is, until one Christmas night, when I decided enough was enough.

I can still picture her face: the bruises on her pale skin, her little body all broken. I walked into the room that night and saw him over her. She was barely hanging on, her breaths shallow, her lips shaking as she whispered my name. I just froze, feeling this mix of rage and fear, but when her eyes locked on mine, something broke.

My little sister died in my arms. I held her tight, her body limp and cold. I didn't know I even had a sister until I found my birth parents, and he—the devil—took everything away.

The axe was *just there* in the garage. He laughed, the creepy kind of laugh that gives you chills, but he stopped when he noticed me holding the axe. The first swing was pure rage. The sound of the blade smashing into his skull was the only thing I heard, and I couldn't stop. I brought it down over and over, sending him right back to hell.

My mother tried to make a break for it, but tears couldn't spare her from justice. I ran after her with the axe, still dripping with blood, until she fell. Her eyes went huge and frightened, and for the first time, I saw her for what she was: a coward.

Her begging meant nothing. I swung the axe, and the house fell silent. Blood pooled at my feet as 'Happy Xmas' by John Lennon played on the radio.

I dropped the axe, my hands shaking profusely, and went to my sister's room. I pulled her lifeless body into my arms and cried until I felt completely empty. Then, I called the only person who would help me: my adoptive father.

Years later, Lyka holds me. All that guilt, all the anger I tried to conceal—it kills me every year. As much as I might want to forget it, the memory taunts me.

I push Lyka aside and wrestle myself up. "I need Flora," I say to him, my voice scratchy. "I just need to hold her."

Lyka rises with me. "Dax, relax for a second."

I don't listen, my legs already carrying me toward the bathroom. Lyka's right behind me, but whatever. All I can think about is Flora. I reach the door and don't bother knocking. I push it open, and it smacks against the wall with a loud thud. Steam billows out to greet us, and there she is, standing in the shower. The water pounds down on her bare skin. She has absolutely no idea we're here—she's in her own little world, softly humming.

The sight of her pulls me away from all those mad things whirling inside my brain. *She is beautiful.*

Her dark blonde hair is soaked and plastered to her skin. It frames her face, and her eyes—one green, one blue—pull me right in.

I can feel a lump well up in my throat, and I'm clenching my fists at my sides, trying not to fall apart.

I walk up, swing open the shower door, and surprise her. She spins around, her eyes going wide when she sees me. For a moment, she's dumbfounded, but that changes fast.

I don't hold back. I tug my shirt off and unbutton my pants, getting rid of everything until I stand utterly naked and exposed. I get under the water, closing my eyes as the warmth hits my skin.

Flora stares at me, her brows scrunching as she scans my face. I try to focus on anything but her, looking down instead. I hope she can't tell I've been crying; I don't want her to find out how weak I am.

She says nothing; she just leans in closer, wrapping her arms around me. Her boobs press against my chest as the water pounds down on us, but all I can feel is her heartbeat against me. My arms wrap around her, holding her tight, as if she's going to disappear. "Dax...you're shaking."

"I'm okay," I manage to get out. "I needed to be close to you, Flower."

She doesn't push. She just holds me, her touch grounding me. And for the first time in what feels like days, the chaos inside me starts to settle.

FLORA

I can tell something is wrong. His eyes are puffy and red, his expression raw.

I've never seen him like this.

A hundred questions come to mind, but the words catch in my throat. Something tells me this isn't a time for questions. His eyes flicker to mine for a second. He tries to conceal it, but I see the pain etched across his face—the weight of something he carries alone. I don't know what happened to him around Christmas, but it's eating away at him.

The shower door slides open once more, and Lyka walks in. He doesn't utter a word. Instead, he hugs Dax from behind, totally completing the embrace. Dax stiffens, stuck between us, but Lyka doesn't let go.

Slowly, I feel Dax relax.

We stand crowded under the running water. This is more than a hug—it's a way we can tell Dax without words that he is safe.

Suddenly, Dax loosens his hold on me without saying a word, letting go. He turns to face Lyka, and they stand there a moment, water pounding down.

Lyka's hand slides up the back of Dax's neck, his fingers wrapping tightly around it, anchoring him. Dax gasps in surprise as he draws him closer until their foreheads touch, their faces inches from each other. I watch them, frozen as they gaze at each other in silence. I can't hear what Lyka says, but his lips move. *I'm here.*

Lyka leans in, brushing his lips faintly against Dax's, the first touch no more than a test. Then, the kiss deepens, their lips crushing together. They both begin to move with more urgency, like they've been starving for this. Dax hands hover awkwardly for a moment, but then, he places one on Lyka's cheek, the touch hesitant yet grounding, as though he's searching for the right way to bridge the unspoken.

I stand close, unable to tear my gaze away.

As they tower over me, the water courses down their bodies, making each muscle and tattoo stand out. They look like they've been carved from Heaven itself—I follow the hard line of the Vs cut into their abdomens down to their hard, commanding cocks.

My heart races. I have never seen them kiss all the times

we've been together, not once. This is different. I'm so turned on, I can hardly think straight. My body feels like it's on fire. Despite the warmth of the water surrounding us, my nipples harden.

Fuck. I can already feel my pussy getting wet, the ache between my thighs growing impossible to ignore.

Lyka's hand stays on Dax's neck, pulling him closer.

I know I should give them some space, but it's impossible. I've never seen either of them this way before. So vulnerable. So open.

I move closer, letting the water splash my face, stinging my eyes. I need to get closer, feel their warmth, and involve myself in this moment. My hands move up their thighs.

Their lips melt into one another, tongues doing a silent dance. Still, I feel the subtle changes in their bodies—the slight turn of Dax's hips, how Lyka does the same. They are inviting me to join. I lower to my knees, wet hair falling around my face, water dripping from my chin. The tiles are freezing against my skin, but I don't care. My main concern is Dax's cock. It stands proud and hard, pushing up against Lyka's side. It has been far too long since I tasted him, and here he is, waiting on me. I can't help but grin as I lean in, my fingers wrapping around the base of his shaft. His skin is wet, but I can feel his pulse underneath, begging for my mouth. Licking my lips, I throw my head back to catch Dax's gaze. His eyes are dark with lust. *I don't want to disappoint him.*

I lick along the length of his shaft from base to tip, real slow. I flick my tongue around his sensitive head, teasing the slit, really savoring the taste of him. He makes a little noise, muffled by the kiss he's still sharing with Lyka.

"Damn," he says against Lyka's mouth, his hips surging forward, as if he wants to delve deeper into my mouth. But I'm not ready for that just yet. I want to make this last, want to stretch out every second of pleasure I can give him.

I lock on to his tip, my tongue probing for that little pearl of pre-cum. It has a salty taste I gulp eagerly. I don't want to waste a drop. My hand grips his base tighter, keeping him steady while I tease him with my tongue. "You taste so good," I manage to say.

Next to me stands Lyka's erect cock, wetted by the same mix of water and pre-cum. His eyes are heavy-lidded, filled with the same hunger I see in Dax. They are both relishing how I worship the two of them. I lick Dax's cock one last time and pull away, leaving him panting against Lyka's mouth. Then, before he can rein himself in, I turn my attention to Lyka, my hand sliding down to wrap around his shaft. His skin is hot, twitching in my grasp as I start to stroke.

"Hmm," I moan. "You look so good...standing there, ready for me."

Lyka whimpers, tugging my head forward. I move closer, inhaling deeply. Then, still smiling, I open my lips, take him into my mouth, and swallow him down. Every inch of Lyka's body jerks, his legs quivering as I start to suck and lick, my tongue roving over him. Dax pulls back from Lyka's kiss and watches, his hand moving to cup Lyka's jaw, keeping him steady while I go to town. He knows what I'm up to. His fingers press into Lyka's skin, his knuckles turning white with the effort. "That's it, Flower," Dax growls. "Just like that. Make him beg for it."

I look up at Dax and catch his eye while I work Lyka's cock with my mouth. The fierce, possessive hunger burning in them makes me tingle. He wants to see me give in to them—wants to watch me completely surrender to their pleasure.

I pull Lyka's cock out with a wet plop and drool down the front of his shaft, smirking up at him. "You like that, Lyka?"

Lyka groans as his head falls onto Dax's shoulder. "I love this... You're such a good girl." I smile, satisfied with his response.

I bring my mouth back down to his cock, but this time, I focus on the tip. I swirl my tongue around it, hitting the ridge with a lot of pressure—just the way he likes it. Lyka gasps, and his body arches off the tile wall.

"Fuck... That feels so good." he breathes, his voice cracking with need.

I hum in the back of my throat, and the vibrations travel down his length. I can feel his cock twitching in my mouth while his legs wobble, even as he tries to hold it together. I love watching him lose his cool, knowing I'm the one driving him crazy.

Lyka fists my hair and tugs my head back, baring my throat. "Good fucking girl," he breathes. "Take it all."

His hips buck forward in a deep groan as he thrusts into my mouth; his cock hits the back of my throat, and I gag. I tremble as I try to keep up, taking him deeper.

"That's it, Flower," Dax growls. "Make my brother come."

My jaw aches with the effort, and my throat is raw, but I can't stop. A slippery mess of saliva and precum drip down my chin. Each thrust pushes more of him into my throat. My body responds to his pleasure—my nipples harden into sensitive peaks and my core tightens. Then, with one last, deep stroke, Lyka comes in my mouth. His moan is loud, reverberating in the shower as I savor the taste.

So perfect.

Dax's hand moves off my hair down to my throat as I release Lyka's cock. "Now it's my turn. Open that pretty mouth again."

I don't even have time to swallow Lyka's cum before Dax enters my mouth.

"So fucking obedient."

My lips wrap snugly around him, and he emits a guttural groan that makes my whole body tingle. I move my head up and down, each time taking him further into my throat.

Dax doesn't care that Lyka's cum covers his cock and seeps from the edges of my mouth. His hands find the back of my head, and his fingers thread through my hair to guide me. I glance up at him, catching his eyes for a brief second, satisfaction flaring through me knowing I'm making him happy.

Lyka's gaze falls to Dax, and he reaches out, his fingers light against Dax's chest before leaning in for a kiss. Their lips collide in a wild, frenzied moment as their tongues twist, fighting for breath.

I focus on Dax's cock. He tugs harder at my hair, his other hand pulling Lyka closer to him. They break apart, both gasping for air, staring at each other. "Damn, her mouth is so fucking perfect," Dax moans.

Lyka smiles that sexy little smile of his. "Fill it with cum, Dax."

My nose rubs against his skin while I move my mouth down his shaft.

Dax makes a raw noise. "I'm so close." He inhales deeply. "I'm gonna fill her mouth with so much fucking cum."

I start working a little quicker now, my lips moving faster along his length, my tongue teasing over the sensitive place underneath his shaft.

Dax moans louder as he leans into Lyka for yet another kiss. I watch them, my arousal growing with each passing second. I can feel the wetness pool between my legs.

I know he's close.

His body tenses, his muscles pull, and he struggles to restrain himself. He is past the point of no return. With one final thrust of his hips, he comes, his release filling my mouth. I swallow quickly, my throat convulsing around him as I take every drop.

Dax falls back on the tiles, and Lyka kisses him once more, both panting, their bodies dripping.

I finally pull back, wiping my mouth with my hand. I shake as my heart hammers in my chest. I look at them, my eyes wide with a mixture of pride and hunger.

"Just what I needed," Dax pants as he pulls me up to join them.

As the water cascades around us, Dax hooks his finger under my chin and tips my head up so our gazes meet.

There's something different in the way he looks at me now. I'm relieved to see some of that heaviness he was holding is lighter, at least for now. His thumb lightly brushes my jaw—a sweet gesture that makes my heart skip a beat.

"We're gonna give you the best Christmas, Flower." It's the way Dax says it—so sure, so certain—I believe him completely.

A smile pops up before I realize it. I cannot imagine celebrating Christmas without them. They are my family—my comfort zone. Dax's lips quiver a little, eyes gleaming with a bit of happiness.

I know I didn't make everything perfect for him, but if I've given him one minute of peace, that's good enough.

Lyka puts a hand on Dax's shoulder and one on mine, anchoring us both. We are just three people standing in the hot, steamy shower, sharing an intimate moment.

This Christmas will be magical.

THREE

LYKA

"SHAKE UP CHRISTMAS" BY TRAIN PLAYS ON THE RADIO AS I CURL UP ON the couch with my hot chocolate, the fire sending wisps of golden light around the room.

All I can do is replay that kiss with Dax in my head. We've never done anything like that, and honestly, it just felt...right. It wasn't about wanting each other or anything physical. I watch Dax and Flora on the sheepskin rug in front of the fireplace. Loads of cardboard boxes surround them, the flaps worn out from age, each filled with old-timey Christmas decorations.

The boxes have not been opened in years—not since we were teenagers. It was a big thing, back in the day, for us to decorate this cabin for Christmas, but life got tougher, and the holidays lost their magic.

Flora bursts out laughing, light and contagious, as always. She holds up a cute little ceramic angel. Even with its wings chipped, it still looks kind of adorable, with childlike round eyes and chubby rosy cheeks.

Beside her, Dax digs into one of the boxes, furrowing his eyebrows as if searching for something. Suddenly, his face brightens, and he pulls out a dinosaur wearing a Santa hat. The green paint has faded in spots, but it's recognizable.

I thought Mom threw that thing away.

"Damn, I haven't seen this since I was a kid," Dax says with utter amazement, spinning the ornament in his hands, examining it like some sort of treasure. He holds it up toward me.

I lean in closer. "How could I forget? You wouldn't shut up about dinosaurs."

He lays the ornament down carefully. Flora frowns and tilts her head to one side, looking perplexed. "Why a dinosaur? I mean, it's cute and all, but it doesn't scream Christmas, does it?"

Dax dramatically gasps, clutching his chest. "Whoa! Dinosaurs were here way before Santa, okay? Give some love to the original legends."

Flora's eyes go big for a second before she starts cracking up. "Guess I can't argue with that," she says between snorts, planting her angel down next to his dinosaur.

Flora suddenly fists some tinsel and smells it.

"What are you doing?" Dax asks, looking confused.

"What? Tinsel has a certain smell."

Wait, does it?

"No, it doesn't…"

"Yes, it does."

Oh lord, they are fighting over whether tinsel has a smell. I pick up a strand and breathe in. "She's right, Dax. Tinsel does have a smell."

Their voices intertwine with the crackling fire, and I kind of zone out. I look above the fireplace, and there's Flora's painting, right in the center. She somehow nailed every little thing about the cabin—every knot in the wood, every shadow from those tall cedarwoods outside. It's stunning, just like her.

I am lost for a second, blown away by her talent. She can see details so crystal clear and deep and turn them into something so beautiful.

The radio jolts me back into reality with a song change. I instantly recognize it.

"So this is Christmas..."

Just like that, the atmosphere changes.

I look over at Dax, and I see it—the clench of his jaw, his body tightening with the first notes of the song. My heart sinks. *Fuck!*

It's that song. He has never really talked about it, but I know it's connected to that night: the night he killed his parents. He breathes rapidly, his hands clenching into fists. He springs up from the rug, crosses the room in an instant, and yanks the radio clean out of its socket. The music dies instantly, leaving a heavy silence in its wake. He growls and tosses the radio at the door. It explodes into smaller fragments, but that still isn't enough. He wrenches the door open and flings the rest of the radio outside into the snow.

Flora sits up straight, her eyes wide with alarm.

"Uhh—" she starts to say, but with a finger, I quickly gesture for her to keep quiet.

Her lips press into a thin line, and she nods, though the concern on her face doesn't let up. She watches as Dax returns to his spot on the rug, his eyes fixed on the fire.

"I hate that song," he growls through his teeth.

Flora glances at me, silently asking for guidance. I shake my head slightly, mouthing *leave it.* She turns her attention back to the decorations.

I keep an eye on Dax. He's all right—things will be fine, but his hands are shaking and his breath is still labored. That song doesn't just bring back memories; it drags him right into the worst of them.

It is time to cheer the cabin up. "We need a Christmas tree," I say.

Flora lights up, her eyes sparkling. "Oh, yes! Should we pop down into town and buy one?"

That's all it takes for Dax to become a whole different person. His jawline relaxes, and I manage to catch the corner of his mouth twitching right before it breaks into a big smirk. His eyes sparkle with laughter.

"What?" Flora says, clearly confused, her brow furrowing as she looks between us.

I set my head in my hand, giving it a little shake as I take a deep breath, trying not to crack up. But Dax gets there first, leaning in and teasing. "Flower...what surrounds the cabin?"

Flora blinks, even more confused for a second. Then, it hits her. Her cheeks heat with a soft pink glow, and she bites her lip. "Trees..."

Dax bursts into a genuinely hearty laugh that fills the entire room. I lean down and peck Flora on the forehead. Her blush deepens at my touch.

"Never change, beautiful."

Flora goes from being embarrassed to just being cheeky in an instant. She stands up, places her hands on her hips, and looks at us as if she is the boss.

"Alright, twats," she says, the slight lilt of her accent catching on the word. "Aren't the trees too big for the cabin?"

"Twats?" Dax repeats. "Wow, that's really British."

Flora huffs dramatically, but a smile tugs at her lips.

"Don't worry," I say, raising an eyebrow suggestively. "I'll make it fit."

Flora frowns, folding her arms over her chest.

"Oh, I've heard that before," she mutters under her breath.

Dax almost rolls on the floor laughing. I can't help it either; my head shakes back and forth as I crack up.

With the sun sinking lower in the sky, the clock is ticking. We have to find the perfect tree before it gets dark. The ATVs' tires crunch on fresh snow as the cold nips at our faces. Flora sits behind me, arms locked around my waist for balance. Dax cruises ahead on his ATV, pulling a small, rattling trailer behind him.

He slows down finally and cuts the engine. We pull over next to him into a small clearing where the trees aren't huge, just right for the cabin.

I hop off the ATV and help Flora down, my hands lingering on her waist a little longer than necessary. She takes a moment to admire the trees as Dax jogs to the trailer to fetch a chainsaw.

"Right," Dax says, smiling. "Let's go find our Flower, the best tree."

We look at all the trees around us. Flora cocks her head and purses her lips in this adorable, thoughtful pout.

"None of them really stand out to me," she finally says, sounding bummed.

Dax rubs his neck and looks to his right. "How about I check out this side?" He points at a small clump of evergreens. "You and Lyka look over that way."

I nod, taking Flora's hand and pulling her the other way. We trudge through the snow, the only sound is the crunch of our boots. Light from the sun throws long shadows, making the forest look warm and magical.

When we are far enough away that Dax can't hear us, Flora slows down, then stops. She leans against the trunk of a big pine tree, staring dead into my eyes.

"Lyka..." she starts, hesitating.

My stomach tightens. *Ugh, I don't like where this is going.*

"Come on," she says, sounding desperate. "I'm seriously begging you. What's up with Dax?"

"Flora, no. That's his story to tell." I make it clear the subject isn't open for debate—or at least, I think I do.

I start to walk away, but she catches my hand. I turn back, and there go those darn puppy eyes, drilling right into my soul.

"You really think that's gonna work?"

She doesn't respond. She looks up at me. Her lips curl a little, and she chews the corner of the bottom one, as if deciding whether to take it further, driving me crazy.

I move another step closer and press my hand on the rough bark of the tree above her head, leaning in enough to bridge the space between us. She looks me up and down, as if sizing me up. "Don't go trying to be all seductive to get me to spill the beans."

She rolls her eyes and lets out a deep sigh. She's having none of it. "Whatever."

Ugh, I fucking hate it when she does that. The tone and the attitude—it sends me out of my mind. My free hand wraps around her throat, my thumb under her jawline. "What did I say about rolling your eyes at me, Flora Faulkner? Don't make me fuck the attitude out of you."

Her eyes go a little wider, but not in fear—nope, it's something else, adding fuel to the fire in my chest.

"Oh, it's been forever since I've seen this side of you," she teases.

I lean in and whisper in her ear. "Remember who's in charge here," I say, letting it sink in. "Now cut the fucking attitude."

"No."

My jaw tightens, and my grip on her throat shifts just enough to let her know I'm not playing around.

"You're really pushing me now," I say with my teeth clenched.

I push her against the tree, the rough bark scratching her winter coat. And then, to my utter surprise, she grins. That fuckin' grin—mischievous and bold.

Do it, she mouths silently.

There's just a little spark of something darker. Part of me wishes she still feared me and still looked at me with those wide, unsure eyes, but she doesn't. She doesn't fear me anymore. She challenges me. In a weird way, it's even more infuriating.

My hand slips from the tree, but I don't retreat. Instead, I lean in. My fingers trail down the bend in her shoulder, grazing her arm before settling at her hip. I move for her pants button, my fingers trying to get it loose.

She doesn't stop me. If anything, her smirk grows, taunting me. She only raises an eyebrow; her lips twitch, as if she is suppressing a laugh.

Damn you, Flora Faulkner.

I yank her pants and underwear down to her ankles. She gasps and pushes her back against the tree even harder.

I quickly slip two fingers into her pussy as she lets out another gasp, whimpering a little.

Fuck, *she sounds perfect. Sing for me, Flower.*

Her arms naturally wrap themselves around my neck, pressing herself closer.

I pull my fingers out and plunge them in deeper this time.

"Lyka!" she cries, her voice shaking with need. I pull them out, stuffing them into her mouth. She sucks them with no hesitation, and the sight makes my cock painfully ache.

"I'm gonna bend you over, and you're gonna grab that tree while you take every inch of me," I tell her. "Just like that first time we fucked, remember?"

I spin her around, dropping my hand to the back of her head, and shove her down, nice and firm. She digs her fingers into the rough bark, holding tight. I admire how her ass curves just right in the sun as I stand behind her.

"Where is the attitude now?" I taunt.

Her bare ass and pussy are on display—I can see the wetness between her legs. I let my pants fall to the ground, and my cock springs free, hard and ready. The cold air strokes its head and causes a shiver to run down my spine. I reach towards her and place my hand over her mouth. "Spit in my hand."

She spits into my palm twice. "That's a good girl."

I scoop it up, feeling the warmth from her saliva as I rub along my shaft.

My erection presses up against her ass. I reach down and rub it along her pussy, feeling her softly moan as her hips rock.

Fuck, I can't wait.

I get my cock ready at her entrance. Without thinking, I grab her hips and dive right in. A cry escapes her that's a mix of pain and pleasure, and I feel her walls clamp down on me.

Her entire body quivers at each strong thrust, but I hook her hips tight, helping her move with me. Our bodies smack together, the sound echoing through the trees.

A memory flashes—the last time we had sex against a tree. The idea of her getting hurt, even in the smallest way, doesn't sit right with me. I take one hand off her hip and grab a fist of her hair, pulling her face off the tree.

She surrenders to me so fucking willingly.

I thrust hard, my cock reaching deeper inside her as she clings tighter to the tree. I feel my orgasm building, tension coiling in my limbs.

With every movement, our winter coats rustle in the silence of the forest.

I have a feeling Dax will burst from the trees any minute. It wouldn't be the first time he has caught us and jumped in, but for now, it's just me and her, completely lost in the moment.

She shudders, her knees buckling a little. I hold her steady, my hand firm on her hips.

"Oh, you're not going anywhere."

"Lyka... "

My cocks hits her G-spot over and over, and I can *hear* her pussy getting wetter.

Thrust.

Slap.

Thrust.

"I'm gonna–" she stutters, out of breath.

"Come," I urge, thrusting harder. "Do it now. Let go, baby."

Her orgasm slams into her like a wave, shaking her as she clings to the tree. Then, she screams my name, her voice echoing through the forest. I feel her pussy clench around my cock, milking me. "Fuck, Flora."

I slam into her one last time, hard and fast, my cum shooting deep inside her as I give her all I have.

I ease up on her hair, letting my hands fall to her hips to pull her closer. I don't want to leave her pussy.

Everything around us blurs out, the forest silent except for our heavy breathing. She still holds onto the tree.

And then, out of nowhere, Dax's voice crashes through the silence. "I turn my back for one second, and you're at it already."

I freeze, my chest still heaving as I whip my head around to find him a few feet off, chainsaw in hand, one eyebrow cocked, a smirk tugging at the corner of his mouth.

Flora tenses up. "Oh my God."

I give Dax a side-eyed look. "Do you mind?"

Dax leans against the closest tree with an amused look on his face. "Not at all. Please, don't let me stop you."

Asshole.

I pull out of Flora, and as I do, the cold air hits the end of my cock. I'm pulsating, body still humming, and I catch a glimpse of cum trickling down the inside of Flora's thigh. But as the thought strikes me to say something, Flora cuts right into the moment.

"Hey, Dax, it's kinda rude to stare," she says, playful yet serious, tugging up her pants.

I can't help but chuckle a little as I hurry to fix myself, zipping up my clothes. When both of us are decent again, I take her hand in mine, interlacing our fingers. I pull her, moving us across to where Dax is lounging against the tree.

As we get closer, Dax straightens, his typical cocky grin on display. Without missing a beat, he strides forward and grabs Flora's cheeks as if he owns them, tilting her face up to his. "Don't worry. I'll be filling you up later, Flower."

Flora's eyes widen, and her lips part like she's going to say something. Before she can, though, Dax leans in and kisses her. For a second, I stare at the two of them.

Their tongues meet, and Flora can't seem to get enough of him.

Dax leaves her breathless, with rosy cheeks. "I think I've found you the perfect Christmas tree."

Without waiting for her reply, he leads her across the snow.

I follow closely, my cock throbbing, dying to be inside her pussy again.

Dax stops in front of a big boulder covered in snow and moss. There stands a proud fir tree, its branches spread out, all symmetrical and full.

Flora gasps, her fingers flying to her mouth for a second before she looks at Dax. "It's perfect, Dax."

Dax grins, lowering the chainsaw to the ground and

fiddling with its controls. "Step back," he says, and the thing roars to life.

She steps closer to me, her hand slipping into mine, fitting as if it belongs there. The hum of the chainsaw cuts through the air, and Flora and I take another step back together as I squeeze her hand.

"I've never had a real Christmas tree before," she says, her lips curling into a shy smile. "We always had a fake one when I was a kid."

"Honestly, there is something magical about the real deal."

The smell of pine and her light perfume hits me. *Fuck, I'm horny.*

Dax angles the chainsaw, making quick work of the trunk. Sawdust flies everywhere but gets whisked away on the breeze.

Finally, the tree groans and falls, coming to rest in the thick snow. Immediately, Flora erupts in a fit of excited laughter.

Dax switches the chainsaw off and brushes wood chips off his gloves. "Perfect, right?" he asks, gesturing to the tree.

"It is. Thank you," Flora replies.

I forget about the cold, snow, and even Dax. The only things that exist are her, her happiness, and the firm feel of her hand in mine.

FOUR

FLORA

We pull up outside the cabin. Most of the snow seems to have fallen off the tree branches during the ride. Already, Dax and Lyka are off their ATVs, untangling the tree from the trailer. I stand there, my breath puffing white in the nippy air.

The snow spreads on the ground like this huge, intact canvas, sparkling in the sunlight. The cabin looks so cozy contrasted against it, and I feel a tightness in my chest from mere amazement. We never had this much snow in Britain. For a day or two, it would sprinkle, like some sugar on the hill, and then slush up. But here it is, thick and soft, endless. Perfect.

"Hey, are you gonna help, Flower? Or are you gonna stand there staring off at nothing?"

I snap out of my daydream at Dax's words. Nothing? Seriously? How is this view nothing? It's everything.

"The snow is super thick here," I say quietly. "It was never like this in Britain."

Dax slides behind me, his gloved hands finding my waist.

"This is still pretty light," he says. "It's gonna get way deeper. We'll be stuck up here for about a month or so."

The words feel like a slap in the face. My heart surges, and my skin grows cold under the layers. Another trick? No, surely not. They wouldn't. They couldn't play that on me again, would they?

It doesn't even register; I just act. I push back from Dax, my heart racing. I start to run, my boots crunching in the snow. My winter gear feels like an anchor, weighing me down with every step, but I keep moving. I have to get away. My throat burns, every gasp like inhaling ice shards. My lungs beg for a break.

"Flora!" Lyka screams from behind me, his voice edged with worry. "Where are you going?"

I look over my shoulder, thinking they'd be right behind me. They stand there, frozen.

I feel my legs give out, and I trip over a fallen tree trunk, the bark scratching my gloves. I drop to the ground, leaning back against the cold wood and trying to catch my breath. Tears stream down my face, hot and unrelenting, blurring my vision. I feel them freeze in the chill of winter's air.

I will never outrun them. I never could. No matter how hard I try, no matter how desperate I get, I will always be their prey. Memories flash through my mind, unwanted and cruel: chains gouging into my wrists, voice hoarse from begging to be freed. each attempt at flight ending in punishment, humiliation, and despair.

I wrap my arms around myself, rocking back and forth as I mutter through my tears, "No. No. They wouldn't do this to me again. They wouldn't..."

But part of me isn't sure. The fear runs deep, mixed in with all the scars they left.

The crunch of the snow catches me off guard. Something drops in front of me, and my head jerks up with a gasp. Teary-eyed, I see them—Dax and Lyka. They are just feet away, looking so worried. I glance down at the snow between us where the cabin keys lay.

Lyka drops to his knees, the snow squishing under him. His steady hands wrap around me, drawing me into his warmth. I can hear real emotion in his voice.

"We couldn't do that to you," he whispers into my ear. "Never again, Flora."

First, I tense, shaking. But eventually, his words crawl through the layers of fear, like sunlight breaking through storm clouds.

Dax drops down beside me. His gloved hand brushes off the snow gathering on me before he tucks a strand of hair behind my ear and lets his thumb linger on my cheek. His brown eyes meet mine, full of regret.

"You can leave whenever you want." He reaches into the snow and snatches the keys up. He shoves them into my hand and wraps my fingers around them. "We can't change what we did to you..." he continues, his voice cracking slightly. "We can't take it back. But we're working on it, Flora. We're really trying."

I look down at the keys and back up to their faces. The snow falls quietly around us, as if the whole world is holding its breath in anticipation. For a moment, I can only hear the whispering wind and my shallow, irregular breathing. My tears start to fall faster, but this time, they are fused with relief. They aren't dragging me back. They're waiting, leaving the choice in my hands.

I don't know why I ran. The memories just flash in my mind like a small voice that refuses to disappear. Lyka embraces me tightly, and I bury my face against his shoulder. I have been with them for many months now. Ever since the ectopic pregnancy, they have been very considerate—super gentle, patient, careful with me.

Still, that fear follows me, creeping into the shadowy corners of my mind.

Lyka carries me through the snow, Dax a few feet behind, quiet and watchful.

"I'll sort the tree out," Dax calls as we near the cabin.

The cabin door creaks open, and a wave of warmth hits me. Lyka walks in and carefully sets me down on the couch. I melt into the cushions, exhausted. He kneels in front of me to unzip my coat before pulling it off. Then, he moves to take off my boots.

"I'm...I'm sorry," I say quietly. My hands fidget in my lap, messing with the fabric of my sweater. Shame nearly consumes me – for bailing, for second-guessing, for letting the past mess up the life we are piecing together.

Lyka's eyes fill with tears. "You don't have to be. I'm sorry you have PTSD because of what we did . We fucked up, Flora. Badly. I know that. I don't blame you for acting the way you did."

What he says hits me much harder than it should.

He leans over and places his hand on my thigh, his thumb tracing small, slow circles.

"We'll do anything to make sure you feel safe with us."

I nod, my throat too tight to speak. His touch lingers another moment before he pulls away, his expression hesitant. "I'm gonna go help Dax with the tree, baby."

I nod again, and he pecks a quick kiss on top of my head before he leaves. My eyelids feel heavy, every emotion from the day weighing them down as I sink deeper into the couch.

A LOUD BANG JOLTS ME OUT OF MY NAP. I BLINK A COUPLE TIMES,

confused as Lyka's voice breaks the silence. "Oh, fuck. That's one bauble shattered."

I slowly lift myself up from the couch, rubbing my eyes and looking around the cabin. . The warm gold firelight flickers, combining with the glitter of string lights. The Christmas tree now stands tall in the corner, bedecked in bright ornaments.

"Oh, look, someone's awake," I hear Dax say from across the room.

I yawn and stretch, taking in the view. Lyka stands on a stool next to the tree, utterly absorbed in hanging an ornament on one of the high branches. Down below him, Dax dangles a garland of tinsel, his head cocking to one side, admiring what they'd done.

"Guess I dozed off," I say, my voice scratchy.

The tree is beautiful—every ornament has been placed with care, from shiny baubles to little homemade things. Multi-colored fairy lights color the room. Lyka flashes a grin. "You needed to catch some zs," he hops off the stool. "We weren't gonna wake you."

Dax throws some tinsel onto the lower branches. "But we couldn't resist showing off," he jokes. "What do you think?"

Cocky fucker.

I look again at the tree. "You guys nailed it."

Lyka wipes his hands on his jeans. "We waited for you to wake up so we could finish the last part." He nods toward Dax, who gets two tree toppers from a box and holds them up for me to see.

"We've got an angel," Dax lifts the fragile porcelain figure with gilded wings, "or a star. You pick, Flower."

I reach toward the angel, her pretty golden wings glimmering in the fairy lights. Dax grins, his face lighting up with pleasure. "That was our mom's favorite."

Lyka sneaks up behind me, wrapping his arms around my

waist before I can utter a word. "Up you go, baby." He lifts me effortlessly, and a small gasp escapes my lips as I balance myself.

"Hey, watch it!" I laugh, stretching up to set the angel on top of the tree.

"Got it?" Lyka asks, his voice straining.

"Yup," I say, totally impressed by how the angel completes the ensemble.

Lyka lowers me to the ground, his hands firm to catch and balance me for a moment.

The three of us stand there and soak it in. The angel seems to watch over us, calm and serene.

My arms instinctively go around their backs, drawing them closer. "I think the tree is missing something."

Dax and Lyka look at each other, confused. "Missing something?" Lyka repeats, tilting his head to inspect the tree.

"What else does it need? It's fucking perfect," Dax adds.

I step back with a smile and head toward one of the boxes on the floor. My fingers close over Dax's favorite dinosaur ornament.

I raise it triumphantly and set the dinosaur on a central branch with care. "You go right here, little buddy. Now it's perfect," I say, stepping back to look at the addition.

A small smile curves Dax's lips. He doesn't say anything, but oh, I can tell by his eyes, I made him proud.

FIVE

DAX

I stir my bowl of venison stew, savoring the taste as I take in the tree. Of all the shiny baubles and blinking lights, the dinosaur ornament stands out.

I take another bite, looking across at Flora. She sits by the fire, the bowl now empty in her lap. Firelight dances across her features, bringing a warm glow to her skin. Lights on the tree sparkle in her eyes too. She is so fucking gorgeous.

But this heaviness in my chest just won't budge. The guilt. It sits there, forcefully reminding me of all the stuff I've done, we've done. No matter how much I want to move on, I can never really forgive myself. I'm broken. I get that.

I tear my gaze from her and look over at Lyka sprawled out on the couch. His long legs stretch out in front of him as he watches the Christmas movie we put on. My mind keeps drifting back to the shower—the kiss.

It was entirely different from other times our lips and tongues had connected. It was deliberate. Real. We have done all that is possible together with Flora in the middle, but a kiss? That's uncharted territory.

Lyka's voice pulls me from my reverie as he rises from the couch.

"I'm all done here." He holds up his empty bowl. "Dinner was good. Appreciate it."

He approaches the fire and bends down, planting a kiss on top of Flora's head. She looks up at him, smiling, and hands him her empty bowl.

Lyka grabs it and raises an eyebrow. "So I guess I'm taking this to the sink, huh?"

Flora bites her bottom lip mischievously.

"Ok, I'm gonna take these, and then I'll be in the barn working on some projects," Lyka says, walking into the kitchen.

"Projects?" Flora asks, curiosity getting the better of her.

I shrug like I don't know.

"No idea," I say, but I can't help smirking a little. Lyka has been working on her Christmas gifts for two months now.

We hear the soft thud as the back door closes behind him.

I slide my bowl across to the side table. Flora lounges on the rug by the fire, completely absorbed in the movie. On a whim, I slide down behind her, settling in with my legs on either side of hers. She leans back ever so slightly, and I sling my arm over her shoulder as my hand finds hers in her lap. I say nothing, lacing our fingers together.

She runs her thumb delicately across the back of my hand before cocking her head slightly to the side. "Not hungry?"

I shake my head.

We sit in comfortable silence. The movie is still playing, but I am too caught up in snuggling with her to pay attention to anything else.

However, I sense tension. I can feel it in the movement, the jitters in her fingers. "Dax..." she murmurs, her voice so quiet, I barely catch it over the crackling fire and movie. There's something about the way she says my name—the fear, the uncertainty—that goes right to my heart.

I glance down at her, my eyebrows furrowing. "What's wrong, Flower?" I ask, my mind racing.

Oh man, is she pregnant? Nah, she's on birth control. But then again, accidents happen, right? And if she *was* pregnant, honestly, it wouldn't be the end of the world. I could get used to the thought of some miniature human running around the cabin—a small version of her beauty and joy, Lyka and me teaching them our ways. I know he wants a child.

The idea seems...nice.

But as I start to dive into that thought, Flora begins fidgeting my fingers.

"Are you okay?" she asks. "You've seemed off these past weeks. Just tell me what's wrong."

Her words shatter the silence between us, and my stomach twists.

Fuck! All right. I really wish this was about a baby.

Hell, it would have been a lot easier. Weighed down by the heaviness of what has been gnawing on me, I have no idea how to put it into words.

I force my eyes to leave hers and lock on the fire, watching the flames as they dance. The heat is insane, almost unbearable, but I really can't look at her right now. It's like the fire is teasing me to just dive right into it and skip what's in store altogether.

"Is it me, Dax?" Her voice breaks just enough to gut me. "Did I do something?"

The words come out harsher than I intend. "No, Flower. It's not anything you did." My hand clenches around hers.

She holds her breath, waiting for me to say something that makes sense. I need to reassure her.

"Uhh..." I start, but then, somehow, I lose my train of thought. I run my hand through my hair, stalling as the words caught in my throat wrestle to get free. I shut my eyes for a second, searching for the guts. "I have been thinking a lot, okay? About my past."

Her fingers tighten on mine, anchoring me in a way I don't deserve. She doesn't pull her hand away. She doesn't interrupt. She just waits.

A wave of fear hits me. After all the stuff I put her through and all the hurt I caused, she wouldn't stick around if she knew the whole truth. She'd be outta here. And I can't let that happen. Not again. Not when she has become my whole world. *She's mine.*

I gulp. "Flora, you promise not to bail on me?" My voice breaks, and my eyes sting with the threat of tears.

She spins around then, utterly attentive to me. When she spots the tears in my eyes, she leans forward and presses against me, her hand nudging my legs. "Move."

My legs sink down on the rug. Then, she swings one leg over mine and sits on my lap, her knees on either side of me. With her thumbs, she wipes away the tears on my cheeks.

"I'm not going anywhere, Dax," she says. "I swear."

Her words are some kind of lifeline, pulling me out of a dark spiral. I close my eyes, leaning into her touch as my hands find their place around her waist.

I don't deserve it. I really don't deserve her.

Please, she better not run... I don't want to keep her here against her will again.

I clear my throat, and the weight of what's next presses down on me. My hands shake slightly as I search for the guts to tell her. "I messed up when I was younger," I start off. "It's about my birth mom..."

Flora doesn't flinch. She simply stares at me, her eyes wide, without a hint of judgment.

"Yeah, she ditched me when I was a baby. I spent years

looking for her. I did everything possible to find her. I needed closure, answers."

Flora lays her hand over mine and gives me a little squeeze.

"When I finally found her, I talked my parents into letting me spend time with her." I stop, struggling to push through the memories assaulting me. "The two weeks I spent with her, well, they were a living nightmare. Terrible things happened—things I never thought I'd survive."

Flora's brow furrows, the lines deepening in concern.

"I killed the bitch!" My voice cracks as I force the words out. "I killed her and my dad, the fucking devil himself!"

Flora's breath catches, but she doesn't move to retreat. Fierce fingers wrap harder around mine, as if to protect me. "Oh, Dax," she says, her voice full of sorrow.

Tears well up in my eyes, and I let them flow. I couldn't hold all this emotion.

"I had my reasons. They weren't good people. He hurt my little sister and me. Every day for two weeks, we went through all kinds of abuse. I used to wake up to the devil touching himself over me and my sister. Then, when I confronted him, he beat me."

The words fly out. I don't even know if I want to look at her, scared of what I may find in her eyes. But she raises her other hand to clear the tears from my face.

Fuck.

The memories were like a freight train, slamming into me hard and fast. "He killed my sister! She was mine!" I scream in a hoarse, raw voice, saliva flying. "He beat her black and blue...until she breathed her last breath in my arms." I clench my fists, the edges of my fingernails piercing my palms. "So, I killed him! I grabbed an axe and killed him! After that, I went after the women who allowed it to happen."

The cabin feels small, the fire too hot, the air fucking thick.

My chest rises and falls, and for a moment, I can't breathe, squashed under the weight of my confession. I'm smothered by the memory, lost in the violence, the desperation, the loss.

Flora grabs my face, pressing our foreheads together. Her cool skin is a balm to the fire raging beneath mine.

She looks into my eyes, firm and steadfast. "I'm here, Dax," she whispers. "I'm here, baby."

Her words cut deep. I kept this pain, this anger, pent up for so long, and letting it out feels like too much.

"That's why I'm such a mess," I sob, my voice breaking. "I ruin everything. Everyone. My adoptive father had to hide the bodies. That's why he started drinking, not because of my adoptive mother dying. It's a lie Lyka and I tell ourselves."

My shame comes out in great, crashing waves.

"I'm fucked up. I've done unforgivable things. Please don't see me differently." My head drops, and I'm a child again, small and helpless, adrift in a sea of guilt and self-hatred. Flora's hands never leave my face. She doesn't speak; she just holds me.

Flora lifts my chin to raise my gaze to hers.

There is no fear or judgment in her eyes, just a calm strength soothing the hurt, aching soul inside me.

"Dax, it's all starting to make sense now. All of it. But I do need to tell you something."

I hold my breath, ready for whatever's coming next.

"I don't see you differently."

I search her face for anything that would suggest she's lying. No, she means it.

The sobs now feel different—not the helpless despair I have carried with me for so long... This is the release I need. I should have told her months ago.

"I guess you don't like Christmas because it happened around then?" she asks delicately, testing the waters.

I once loved Christmas. Images flash—Lyka and me as kids, opening our gifts, laughing at the silly jokes my adoptive father would tell over turkey dinner. Christmas used to be my favorite time of year—until I found *them*.

"It was two weeks before Christmas. I remember getting a gift for my sister—not for Christmas, but for her birthday." I hug Flora closer, really needing her there with me. "Her birthday was on Christmas Eve. That's why they called her Eve."

"Oh, Dax," she says, her tone full of emotion. "I wish you'd told me sooner."

My face burrows into her shoulder. "How could I? That's the kind of shit you take to the grave. I was scared you would run. I can't lose you."

She draws back to cup my face once more, her eyes locking with mine with the usual intensity that makes my chest ache.

"You did what you had to do. They deserved it." She kisses my cheek. "You will never lose me. Do you think after everything, I'm going to run now? Yes. I have my moments, but... " She hesitates. "I love you."

The words hang in the air, and for a second, I literally feel my heart stop. *Fuck.*

She's never said that, not ever.

Oh, man! Breathe!

I guess she notices the surprise on my face, because she gives me one of those little uncertain smiles.

"I love you, Dax," she reiterates, then adds, "and Lyka, of course."

Those few words, so simple yet so powerful, ring in my head, mingling with the doubt and guilt that have haunted me for so long. *She loves me. She loves us.* How can she after everything I just told her? After what we've done to her? After all I've done?

"You...you really do love me?" I gasp, my voice breaking once again.

"Yeah, Dax. I really do. I love you, and I love Lyka."

I've spent so long believing I am unlovable, and here she is, proving me wrong.

"I'm not worthy of you, Flower," I whisper against her skin, shaking.

"You deserve love, Dax. You and Lyka, and you've got mine." I start kissing her chest, but she pulls back. "Baby, please don't ever think you're a monster. Your parents deserved it. After what they did to you and your sister, they got exactly what they deserved."

It's like she can read my mind. I do think that.

In that instant, it's like she can see the man I want to be, not the monster I fear I still am. "You did some messed-up stuff to me, but you also killed for me. I'll never forget that."

We have crossed so many lines, got blood on our hands, all to keep her safe, and now, she's here.

"I know you and Lyka would do anything for me, and that's the reason I love you."

She is right. I would do anything for her.

"I love you so much, Flora Faulkner. Please never leave me," I whisper, my voice choked with emotion. "Please...please don't go."

We stay wrapped in each other for what feels like forever, the fire crackling softly in the background.

I LIFT MY HEAD OFF FLORA'S CHEST AND WIPE THE LIGHT SWEAT FROM my forehead. My brain's a ball of fuzz. The warmth from the fire and her soothing presence put me in a deeper rest than I thought. "Crap," I say, blinking hard a few times to shake off the fog. "Was I really asleep?"

Flora chuckles slightly, teasing, "Yeah, you totally were. Then you started snoring into my chest, you cutie."

My face heats up as I groan, embarrassed. "I don't snore..."

"You do," she shoots back, still grinning. "But I didn't wanna wake you. You looked peaceful for a change. It's been a while."

She tries to pull herself from my lap, bracing her hands against my shoulders, but before she does, I grasp her hips, knowing full well she can stay right where she is.

"Hey, where are you off to, Flower?"

She raises an eyebrow at me, caught somewhere between amusement and disbelief.

"Aren't your legs numb?"

They are kind of numb, but I'm not thinking about that. The way she is pressed against me, her warmth and her scent mixing with that faint pine and fire in the air—it's getting to me in a way I can't ignore.

Fuck, I'm horny.

"They're fine," I whisper, holding her hips tightly. "Just stay."

I give her no room for questions. I lean in, pressing my lips to the soft curve of her neck, and feel her breath catch against me.

I bury my lips into her neck, real nice and slow as I take my sweet time, guiding the swaying of her hips to move with me. Fingers digging into the bend of her waist, I rock her back and forth, that heat plunging through me.

"Dax," she breathes.

"You feel so freaking good. I need to be inside you."

The way her body responds to mine, the minute alterations in the way she moves—it's enough to make me lose my mind.

The firelight throws dancing shadows around us while the heat between us builds.

Flora starts moving against me faster, her hips swaying in a way that makes me release a low groan. I can feel my cock grow hard.

She gasps for air, her lips falling open, and she looks at me with eyes half-closed.

I reach under her tank top. My fingers brush her skin, and I tug the shirt upwards. She arches her body some to give me better access. I toss it over my shoulder before my eyes take in her full breasts.

Her nipples are such a pretty shade of pink.

"No bra?" I tease.

She gives me a small, shy smile, her face flushing, but she says nothing.

I can't resist. I bend down, kissing her breasts. My hands reach for her sides, holding steady as I kiss my way down her skin. She gasps, her fingers tangling quickly into my hair as I start moving lower.

I rain kisses down her nipples until I finally pop one in my mouth and swirl my tongue around that sensitive little peak. She moans, arching her back slightly. My other hand reaches for the opposite breast, my thumb rubbing over that hard bud, which makes more sounds spill from her.

Her reactions drive me wild, and I move my mouth to her other nipple, giving it just as much attention. Every single lick is a new way to claim her, to show her just how much I want her. I dig my fingers into her hips, keeping her moving.

"Dax... Dax..." Flora chants my name breathlessly, her chest rising and falling, her fingers digging into my shoulders.

The way she says my name—it's the only word in the world that makes my head spin.

I pull back just enough to catch her eyes, hands still holding her hips. "Let's get these shorts off." Not a question, a command.

She pauses for a second before getting up. My hands move with her, trailing down her sides as she stands. My fingers catch the waistband of her shorts and underwear.

I yank them down, sliding them over her thighs, stopping at her ankles. She steps out of them, leaving her naked body completely open to me.

The firelight dances across her; my eyes trace down, and I can't help but gulp a sharp breath. Her pussy glistens in the light. Just the view of it gets my blood racing and my cock throbbing with need.

"Damn," I murmur, pulling her closer to me. The firelight flickers behind her, making every curve and inch of her look almost unreal. She is gorgeous, absolutely fucking stunning, and she is all mine.

My eyes locking with hers, expressing the longing and gratitude I can't keep inside me. "Come here, Flower. I need to taste you."

I tug her closer.

Her legs fall open so easily, she pushes herself against my shoulders to maintain her balance, her breathing already catching in anticipation.

I lean in further as my hands glide up her thighs. I take my sweet time—my lips barely touch the inside of her thigh, and her hips move, as if she's beckoning me closer.

I stick my tongue out and lick her slit slowly. *Oh, that sweet, intoxicating taste.*

My hands catch her thighs to steady her while my tongue delves into her with long, slow strokes.

"Fuck," she cries out.

I keep going. I run my tongue over her clit in circles, gauging her reaction. She presses against me, breathing heavier. Every little noise she makes drives me wild, and I'm all about making her feel as good as possible.

I need to go easy. It has been a few weeks since I was last in her pussy. I understand perfectly well that if I rush, I won't be able to hold out.

I'm taking my time, letting my tongue do its thing as I switch it up between slow, teasing licks and firmer pressure.

"You taste so fucking good," I whisper to her. I can feel her juices flowing with each second.

I watch as her head leans back an inch or so, her mouth falling slightly open, letting go completely.

"Dax... Dax, I'm going to—" she says in a trembling voice.

Now, I really give it to her—harder and faster.

I keep going, sliding my hand up her thigh, teasing her entrance with my fingers until, finally, I push two inside her. Immediately, she constricts around me, hot and wet, and I groan against her clit.

I curl my fingers, aiming to reach that sweet spot inside her, and then I immediately transition to a pumping rhythm. Her body bucks against me as her moans grow louder and more insistent.

"Yes! Yes! Just like that!" she yells, her voice breaking, fingers tugging at my hair. "Fuck!"

Her hips buck wildly, grinding against my mouth as she lets it all go. The shaking of her thighs, the shuddering of her whole body, wave after wave of pleasure hitting her—I don't stop, steady in my motions, until she's riding her orgasm as her moans morph into breathless whimpers.

Finally, her body sags, and I withdraw my fingers, pressing kisses against her inner thighs. "That's my good little flower."

She falls onto the rug beneath us, breathing hard, her face red from that incredible moment. I can't help the slight smile that crosses my face as I look at her.

I lean in and wrap my arms around her, lifting her. She's completely limp in my arms, melting into me as I pull her in, kissing her.

"Taste yourself," I whisper against her lips.

Our tongues touch and dance against each other. I can still taste her—the sweetness of her juices on my lips.

Flora moans into my mouth while her hands get tangled in my hair as our kiss deepens. I let my tongue flatten over hers for a moment, and then I pull away, leaving her panting for more. "I need more of you. I need to lick you clean."

I take her wrist and tug her down onto the rug. *She trusts me.*

"Head down," I tell her. "Pussy in the air for me."

She folds onto all fours without a word. Her head drops onto the rug as her arms stretch out.

Fuck! Her pussy is beautiful.

It makes me salivate. I can see the cream oozing from her.

I go down on my knees behind her and take in the view. My hands move down her back, tracing the bend of her spine, coming to rest on her hips.

I lean and press my lips against her backbone. They trace down to her ass as I spread her.

Without wasting a moment, I plunge my tongue into her entrance, making her bite down on the rug as she moans.

Her body jerks as I lap up her juices. "Let me enjoy you, Flower," I murmur against her, pulling my mouth away.

I taste everything, every ounce of her—ugh, it's fucking incredible. Her loud moans echo around the cabin—I'm surprised Lyka hasn't busted in to see what's going on.

Her body shudders at my touch; her hips grind against my mouth, but it's just not cutting it. *Damn, I've got to be inside her.*

Reluctantly, I pull back, my mouth slick from her arousal. She whimpers as if she doesn't want me to stop. I kneel, my body still shaking as I fumble with my clothes, hauling off my T-shirt and shoving down my jeans. Lying back on the rug, I prop myself up on my elbows.

"Ride me," I instruct.

She lifts her head, out of breath, peering back at me over her shoulder as her lips curve into a cheeky smirk. "Bossy tonight, aren't we?"

My eyebrow arches. I am completely turned on, my cock hard and veiny. "Don't keep me waiting, Flower... "

She giggles, but it's plain as day that she is ready, eagerly crawling toward me. When she's above me, my heart races. "Reverse cowgirl," I tell her.

She does a complete turn, showing me her back. The swaying of her hips as she readjusts sends my breath away. I can't contain myself any longer, reaching out and slapping her ass. She lets out a little squeak of surprise.

She gains her confidence as she gets comfortable. Her feet relax on either side of my thighs, and she balances herself with my legs, lowering herself slowly—inch by excruciating inch.

I clench my teeth, my fists balling at my sides, trying to hold it together. Her wetness brushes against the tip of my cock, and I'm using every ounce of willpower not to thrust my hips upward into her.

Dude, come on, get it together! Two fucking weeks since I've been in her pussy! FUCK!

She's in no hurry. She tortures me as she lowers herself further. Her pussy engulfs my tip, and the heat and tightness send a loud groan tearing out of me as my head falls back onto the rug.

"Flower," I whisper.

Literally, every minute is a fight. My hands are on her hips, tight, wanting to yank her down faster, but I force myself to remain still and let her have her way with me.

"Slowly," I remind her.

She goes down just a bit more, taking me a little bit deeper, her walls clamping down on me, and I feel like I might burst.

She takes all of my cock. I lean in, my hand on her lower back, pressing, urging her to lean forward. Immediately, she's going for it. She grabs my lower legs, and that new angle has me seeing stars. *Fuck.* The sight of her, her back arched, her ass tilted up toward me—a picture is worth a thousand words, they say.

"Sorry if I come quickly," I say, my chest heaving, heart racing, trying to keep it together. "You feel so damn good."

She doesn't say a word. I mean, she doesn't have to.

Instead, she moves, lifting her body. I feel every inch as she slowly, deliberately moves up and slides back down. I shut my eyes, my head tipping back as a low groan escapes me. She quickens the pace—deeper and smoother. The slapping of her skin against mine reverberates through the cabin, joined by my needy whimpers.

There's no way I can hold it back. I really don't want to finish so fast. I want to enjoy this moment longer.

I'm desperate, so I grab her hips, taking control. I have a firm grasp, and with each thrust up into her, I let my momentum increase until her moans are full-fledged yelps of pleasure.

"Ever heard of the game Buckaroo?" I manage to say.

She laughs in surprise then moans as her hands clamp onto my legs, pressing tighter as I move my hips. The angle has me going deeper and harder, her body clamping down on me, pulling me closer to the edge.

My thrusts become erratic and desperate.

"Fuck, I'm coming... I'm com—" I whine as I thrust into her one last time.

The release overtakes me—my muscles tense, and then just about a million waves of pleasure crash over me. I hold on to her hips, keeping her in place. Then, guilt strikes. "I'm sorry, I didn't mean to come so quickly... You just felt so damn good, I couldn't help it."

Flora looks over her shoulder, huffing and puffing, her face red and wet with sweat, her chest rising and falling. I can feel my cum slowly leaking from her, collecting at the base of my cock where we remain joined.

Then, in an instant, she leans back against me, her body weight resting completely against my chest. Her head nestles against my shoulder, and my cock slips out.

I peck a kiss on her cheek before wrapping my arms around her, hugging her tight. The only sound filling the room is now the soft crackle of the fire. I close my eyes for a second, relishing the sensation of having her in my arms.

"You're amazing, Flower. I love you."

"I love you too, Dax."

Her hand comes up on my arm. We lay on the rug, out of breath and all tangled up.

SIX

LYKA

I LEAN AGAINST THE FRAME OF THE BACK DOOR OF THE CABIN, TWISTING the lid of my weed grinder with aching hands. My fingers seem to be locked in place after hours of sanding. It will be worth it, though.

I think about the presents I have been making for Flora recently. I really have put so much thought and effort into each one. I hope they show her how much she means to me. *Fingers crossed she loves them.*

I go to dump the weed onto a thin wrapper. I've cut down to one joint a night, but tonight, the old routine just feels necessary.

Once rolled, I put the joint to my lips, lighting it with a flick of my lighter. The paper crackles, and the first inhale sends a wave of calm through my chest, easing the tension in my shoulders. I let out a breath, watching the smoke swirl into the winter air.

The snow reflects the moonlight, illuminating the back of the cabin in a soft, silvery light.

I guess Dax and Flora are fast asleep. I've been in the barn all night.

I look down at my hands and see the calluses and little cuts, testifying to all the time that has gone into crafting her gifts. My thumb runs across one sore spot, and I grimace for a second.

It's nothing compared to what Flora has had to cope with. I lean against the doorframe and take another drag.

I hear the floorboards creak behind me, breaking the silence, and I turn to see Dax standing in his underwear. He nods to me casually and walks over. I hold the joint out to him.

After he takes a drag, he puffs a ring of smoke into the night. "You finished your projects?"

"Yup, and not gonna lie, they look amazing." The mere thought of Flora's reaction tightens my chest.

Dax nods, takes another puff, and hands the joint back to me. He leans against the doorframe, shifting from foot to foot, the chill creeping in on him. He looks out toward the snowy yard, but it's clear his head is elsewhere.

"I told Flora..." he begins, trailing off.

The joint pauses halfway to my lips, and his confession takes me by surprise. "You did? What did she say?"

"She didn't," he finally says, sounding shocked. "She just... held me."

His words come with the force of a sledgehammer, and for an instant, there is nothing but silence. I'm blown away—just like he is, judging from the look on his face.

I bring the joint to my lips and take a long drag, letting his words sink in. As I exhale slowly, I glance in his direction. He still stands with a rigid posture, though he wants to come off as casual. "That's something, huh?" I prompt, not really knowing what else to say.

Dax nods a little, rubbing his bare arms. "Yeah. It's something."

I can understand how much her acceptance means to him.

The silence between us speaks volumes until Dax finally speaks. "She told me she loves me, Lyka."

She really said that to him?

I swallow hard, trying to avoid the pang of jealousy. There's a part of me that wanted to hear those words first. You know, like wanting to be the person she trusts enough to say them to. But hey, it is what it is. *Flora loves him—of course she does.*

"That's deep, dude," I say, my voice quiet.

Dax shifts a little, running his hand through his hair. "I said it back."

I nod, tucking a small smile at the corners of my mouth against the lump in my chest. "Good," I say, and I mean it. He needs to feel loved after everything we've been through; he is entitled to that as much as I am.

Dax leans in closer, putting his hand on my shoulder. "Hey, don't stress. She said she loves you too."

All I can do for a moment is look at him as a wave of relief washes over me. *She loves me too.*

Dax squeezes my shoulder before he steps back. That moment hangs between us. We don't have to speak to know we're on the same page—how lucky we are she decided to love us, no matter what.

I fling the finished joint out the door. It glows briefly before disappearing into the snow. The door swings shut behind me, and I catch Dax before he walks away.

"We gonna talk about what happened in the shower?" I say.

He freezes mid-stride before pivoting to face me, his face a mask.

"It just happened in the moment, right?" I move closer until there's no space between us, and my heart thumps loudly in my chest. "Right?" I ask him, my hand reaching to his face for a hint —an answer, a nod, anything.

Dax doesn't move, but his eyes lock on mine. His jaw clenches. *What are you thinking, Dax?*

I have no idea how or why, but our lips find their way back together, the spark all too real again. The kiss is hungry. Instinctively, my hands move to cup his face, my thumbs brushing the stubble along his jaw. Dax's hands find my waist, pulling me to him, his fingers biting into my sides.

And before I can even think, he shoves me back, my lower back hitting the edge of the kitchen counter. *What in the name of all that is holy are we doing?*

We both cut the kiss short. Yet, I'm panting like crazy, still holding his shoulders. "We can't," I tell him. "It just doesn't feel right. Not without Flora."

The words hang in the air between us, and I can almost recognize the regret flashing in his eyes. He steps back, running his hand through his hair before pinching the bridge of his nose.

"Yeah, you're right. Fuck, I'm sorry," he grumbles.

The air hums from the unspoken feelings neither of us knows how to handle. I take a step back, putting some space between us, and lean hard against the counter, trying to get my bearings. "Let's not make things more complicated," I throw in.

Dax nods, but his eyes tell a different story.

THE CABIN IS QUIET THIS MORNING AS I WANDER THE KITCHEN. IT smells of cinnamon, nutmeg, and sugar—just like a bakery. I woke up early, as tomorrow is Christmas Day and I want to prep. Dax is probably the better cook, but I wanted to take this on myself.

A stack of golden pancakes sits on a plate, waiting for Flora. I look at them, feeling rather proud of the effort. *Oh, it's the thought that counts.*

I take the gingerbread men out of the oven, the tray smoking while I fiddle with the glove.

"Hot… Fucking hot," I mutter, steadying the tray on the counter.

"Hey, Chef," a voice teases from behind me.

I turn and see Flora lounging in the doorway, wearing one of my big t-shirts and her shorts. Her hair is tousled, her eyes heavy with sleep. "Good morning, baby."

She walks over, stands on her tiptoes, and pecks me on the lips.

I push the plate of pancakes toward her as she takes a seat at the kitchen island.

"Made you some pancakes," I say with a great deal of pride.

Instead of diving in, she shoots me an awkward look. Her lips press together while she thinks about it. "Thank you, but I'm not hungry…"

I raise an eyebrow.

"Hey, don't make me feed them to you," I say jokingly, poking a finger in her direction for effect.

Her expression changes into something sharper as her eyes narrow. "I think we're past that now."

In an instant, there's real tension where playfulness was before. I can feel my throat constrict with the guilt welling up. I really didn't mean anything, but I get why my comment hit a nerve.

"Sorry about that. I was just playing around. I meant nothing by it."

Her face softens a little, and she places her elbows on the kitchen island.

"Well, the pancakes are here if you change your mind," I say, turning my attention back to the gingerbread.

I bend down and snag a bowl from the cabinet. I measure everything for the next batch before I begin mixing, the spoon scraping the sides of the bowl.

"Need help?" Flora asks, breaking my concentration.

Nodding, I invite her to come over.

I inch in a little more as she steps in front of me, letting my chest just press against her back. I reach around and put my hands over hers on the spoon.

"Like that," I softly tell her.

She instantly erupts into giggles when I try to pour a little scoop of flour into the bowl, but it puffs upward before landing on the counter.

"Oh no! Looks like we've made a mess," she says.

With a big grin, I stick my finger into the bowl and scoop up some batter. Before she can say anything, I put a little dab right on the tip of her nose, leaving a cute blob of dough there.

"Aye!" she says, turning in my arms so she's facing me, narrowing her eyes in mock threat.

She sticks her finger in the batter and smears a great big glob on my cheek. "Back at ya!"

I wipe the batter off my face, grinning.

"You better watch it, Missy."

Our hands are covered in batter, but I don't care. The moment draws us closer, our laughter dying as the playful atmosphere dissolves into something more intimate. Our lips meet in a slow kiss that gradually deepens.

Her hands find my face, her fingertips brush against my jaw. The batter is cold on my skin as she holds my cheeks. I mirror her movements, cradling her face with my own messy hands.

When she finally pulls away, her face is flushed. I cannot

help but shoot her a smile as I take her in—the smudges of batter against her cheeks, across her nose.

"Yup, you've got batter all over your face."

A sweet smile breaks across her lips as her eyes lock with mine. She leans in and whispers the words I long to hear.

"I love you, Lyka."

The whole world freezes. My heart races, thumping against my ribs as I process what she just said. I spent all night thinking about how I wanted to say it to her first, practicing the moment in my head, but she totally surprised me.

I lean in, rubbing my thumb over her bottom lip. I take a moment, savoring it.

"I love you too, Flora."

Her phone vibrates then, really killing the vibe. She sighs, digs it out of her pocket, and looks at the screen.

"Ugh, it's Rachel," she mutters.

She answers, walking to the other side of the kitchen. I go back to mixing the gingerbread batter, but I can't help listening. She sounds so official.

"Hey, Rachel," Flora pauses. "I totally understand..."

Ugh, Rachel. The new girl at the bar. She's always off sick, so I don't think this time will be different. I can see where this is going.

"Honestly, you get better. I can manage it," Flora says patiently.

Fucking called it! I grasp the spoon a bit tighter. That leaves Flora stuck covering the bar alone because Nancy's out of town for Christmas. It irritates me Flora's always the one picking up the slack.

Flora hangs up and looks at me, her face saying it all before she even mutters a word.

"Rachel called in sick and you're covering for her, huh?" I reply, knowing the answer.

She nods, blowing out a small sigh.

"Yup. But the good news is, because it's Christmas Eve, I'll be closing early." I can't fight this knot in my stomach. I don't like her working alone, especially this time of year, when the bar might get rowdy.

I put the bowl down, wiping my hands on a kitchen towel.

"Dax and I still gotta finish getting ready for tomorrow," I say, really trying to play it cool. "You can take my truck, and we'll swing by the bar later to see how you're doing. Sound good?"

"Sounds perfect."

She looks down at her hands, all sticky with batter, and laughs.

"I should clean this off." Just before heading out of the kitchen, she leans over and pecks me on the cheek. "Thanks, Lyka," she says.

I watch her leave for the shower, and the knot in my chest pulls tighter. I know she can handle herself, but it doesn't stop me from worrying.

SEVEN

FLORA

I DRIVE DOWN THE SNOWY ROAD, HOLDING THE WHEEL TIGHTER THAN usual. I've never driven in snow before—fortunately, the truck handles it like a pro. Dax outfitted the truck with winter tires and put sandbags in the bed to weigh it down. They helped with the traction, Dax explained. I'd never had to do that in Britain.

Holiday songs play on the radio, but I barely hear them. My mind won't stop thinking about last night and what Dax had told me, of his voice and the pain in it.

I just held him. That was all I could really do.

How could his dad do that? And his mom—how could she do nothing? It's crazy to think about, but that was his life. I don't totally blame him for what went down. Who could? He did what he had to do to make it, even if it meant living with that choice for the rest of his life.

Everything about him finally adds up. I wonder if his adoptive parents ever considered taking him to therapy. Probably not. They sound like the type who'd want to avoid it all—sweep it under the rug. But that kind of trauma doesn't just disappear. I thought I had it hard, losing my mother and father, but damn.

I want to be there for him, to protect him from all the demons he fights in his own head. I pull into the bar's parking lot, grateful the snow has been cleared.

I park the truck and chill for a second, my hands still on the wheel as I let out a deep breath.

I really don't feel like doing this shift.

All I wanna do is hang out at the cabin with Dax and Lyka, soaking up the holiday vibes.

At least I get to shut up early. I cross my fingers, hoping the locals decide to stay home tonight and spend time with their families instead of hitting the bar.

I reach for my bag and hop out of the truck, the cold nipping at my cheeks. *I just wanna get this over and done with.*

A FEW HOURS INTO MY SHIFT, THE BAR IS DEAD. THE ONLY GUY IN THE place is the same old dude who comes in every day. He orders two beers and a bowl of nuts to watch whatever game happens to be on the screen. He was chillin' in his corner, nursing his second drink. I don't know his name, but he has never been a hassle.

I wonder about his life—family? friends? Will he be alone this Christmas? Or is this of his a sort of time-out from something else?

I snatch a towel and head toward his table, wiping down nearby surfaces as an excuse to get closer. His empty bottles line up at the edge, so I reach for them to break the silence.

"Merry Christmas," I say.

He looks up at me, startled, and gives a small, warm smile.

I mean to walk away, but a small voice inside insists I stay.

Stay. Say a little more. So, I turn toward him.

"What's your name?" I ask.

"Uh...my name is Floyd," he says at last, drawing out the words.

"Floyd, would you like another beer? On the house, my friend. It's Christmas!"

He shakes his head, chuckling a bit. "No, it's all right, thanks. I probably should be on my way."

He gets up, puts his flat cap on his head, and ambles to the door.

Something gets the better of me again, and I yell after him, "You're not on your own this Christmas, are you?"

He stops one hand on the door handle and turns back with a good-humored smirk. "I'm not, but thanks for asking. I just come in to watch some sports in peace. I have three women at home—wife, daughter, and granddaughter. Sometimes, a guy just needs a break."

I burst out laughing at his honesty. "Ahh, I see."

"Merry Christmas to you too," he says, tipping his cap in courtesy as he disappears in the snow.

The bar goes quiet when he leaves. If nobody shows up in the next five minutes, I plan to lock up early.

I glance around the bar and observe the few Christmas decorations Nancy threw up. A few strands of tinsel hang lazily across the bar, a small plastic tree sits shoved in the corner with random ornaments—it is obvious she is not really into the holiday spirit. Guess heading somewhere warm was how she chose to celebrate.

I head behind the bar to shut everything off, but just as I reach for the switches, the door swings open.

Laughter and loud voices shatter the silence as people enter, super rowdy and too hyped for my taste. *Ugh, it's Dax and Lyka's so-called friends.*

Tammy, Sav, and Lina walk toward a booth. The girls really get on my nerves with their shrill giggles. I don't want to see them—not now I know they've all slept with Dax and Lyka—but it is what it is. Dax and Lyka are loyal to me now, and quite frankly, that's good enough.

The men make a beeline for the pool tables, Jack and Dickie already fighting.

Sav is the girl I caught Dax with on the couch before we started sleeping together. She tosses her coat on a booth seat like she owns the place. With a sideways glance in my direction, she snaps her fingers.

"Beers for everybody," she orders.

I clench my teeth but keep my cool. *Self-entitled bitch.*

I grab a bunch of beers from the fridge and place them on a tray.

With a clatter, the bottles go down onto the table as I do my best to ignore the eyerolls and whispered gossip.

"Merry Christmas, Flora," Tammy teases. *I can't believe I kissed her once.*

I force a big smile and turn back to the bar. I don't want to deal with them any more than I have to. Usually, Rachel or Nany handle them.

The girls hold onto their beers and make their way over to the pool table. I can sense their eyes darting toward the bar.

I pull out my phone, pretending to scroll; the screen is blank as I tap at it aimlessly. I just need something to do—something to keep me from making eye contact.

Suddenly, the unmistakable crash of a glass bottle sounds through the air.

"Oops..." says Sav, falsely apologetic.

The whole group bursts out laughing. I grip my phone harder, my nails digging into the case. And yeah, there it is: a smashed beer bottle glinting in the lights. *Did she do that on purpose?*

I reach behind the counter for the dustpan and brush. I try to keep a straight face as I approach the mess, but just as I approach it, Jack steps in front of me. Standing all wide and stubborn, he crosses his arms, smirking. He doesn't say one word; he just stands there, totally blocking my path.

I stand still for a moment, weighing whether to push past him or turn back. Before I can do either, a voice rings out from behind, clear and commanding. "Move the fuck out of her way."

I spin around, my heart racing, as I catch Lyka and Dax at the door.

Lyka looks serious, his jaw all tight, while Dax checks the room before his gaze finally falls on me. I can't help it—I bite my lip as a little smile sneaks onto my face. A huge wave of relief hits me. *My men.*

Jack quickly steps aside, the little confidence he had evaporating as he mumbles under his breath. Dax wastes no time darting beside me.

"Hey, Flower," he says, dropping down to get the dustpan. "Let me help you with that."

I look up at him, meeting his gaze and mouth. "Thanks."

He shoots me a small, reassuring smile before letting the shards drop into the trash. The group at the pool table is silent now, the soft clacking of the balls replacing their laughter.

Now the mess is cleaned up, we return to the bar. Lyka leans against the counter, crossing his arms, watching the group. Dax stays beside me. I can finally relax.

"Drinks?" I ask Dax and Lyka, breaking the silence.

They stare at each other a second and then let their guard down, sitting on the bar stools in front of me. "Nah," Dax says with a casual shrug. "We were just stopping by, before getting the turkey. However, seeing who's here, I wanna stay for a bit."

I wrinkle my nose at the word turkey, even as I try to keep my expression neutral. I can tell they notice my reaction, though, because they glance at each other before turning back to me.

"What's up? Don't you like turkey?" Lyka asks, an eyebrow cocked.

I shake my head and bite my nails nervously. "Can't we have beef instead?"

"Beef?" Lyka bursts out laughing. "On Christmas?"

But before I can reply, Dax jumps in, "Hey, whatever my Flower wants, she gets," he says, giving Lyka a little nudge with his elbow.

"Sorry," I say, rushing to explain. "I just think turkey is super dry. It's overrated."

Lyka sighs and shakes his head. "Beef," he repeats under his breath.

Dax leans onto the bar, laughing. "No need to apologize. Beef it is."

The group gets boisterous again. Tammy and Sav are the worst, laughing like they're trying to get Dax and Lyka's attention.

Sav walks over to the bar, Tammy on her heels.

"Hey, Dax..." she says, her voice sweet as she leans in closer to him.

I hold onto the counter, trying not to roll my eyes. *Of course, they wanted Dax and Lyka's attention.*

Tammy floats to Lyka's side, angling her body toward him like she's still trying to ignite some flame.

"Hey, Flora. Two beers, please," Sav says, nice now that Dax is in earshot. *But let me tell you, he's mine.*

Dax edges away from her.

"How's it going, Dax?" Sav asks with big, wide eyes.

I can tell from the stiffening of his shoulders that he feels awkward, but my heart swells at his words. "I'm good. Can't wait to spend Christmas with Flora."

Dropping my name like that—just laying claim and not giving a crap about Sav—is beyond brilliant. I totally love him for that.

I grab the beers from the fridge and slam them on the counter. Maybe Sav and Tammy will get the message and go back to their game.

Unfortunately, Tammy cannot resist trying her luck. She gulps her beer and leans toward Lyka.

"Feels like forever since I last saw you," she says to him.

Lyka doesn't even bother to look at her when he says bluntly, "I've been busy."

Just three short words, spoken in his no-nonsense manner. I can't help but smirk at how grumpy he can get with people he doesn't care for. Tammy falters as Lyka leans away and turns his attention to me.

Sav and Tammy exchange a look of surprise—the cold shoulder has really thrown them. *Good.* Maybe now the message will sink in and they will return to the pool table, where they belong.

Sav and Tammy don't say another word but turn toward the jukebox. A moment later, I hear the first strains of "Santa Baby" by Kylie Minogue, and I mentally groan.

They both grab pool cues and proceed to dance with them, holding them like stripper poles. They sway their hips and run their hands up and down the cues, as if they're putting on a show.

Ugh. They look so desperate. Of course, Jack and Dickie are just eating it up, clapping and cheering like a couple of frat boys.

Dax or Lyka don't play into their little game. Dax keeps his eyes on me while Lyka leans on the counter, unbothered.

"Do you want us to hang around? Wait for you to close?" Dax asks.

"It's okay. You guys get on with your Christmas shopping. I'll catch up with you back at the cabin."

Lyka gives me a look for a second, like he's debating whether to bail.

"Alright," he says finally. "If you need us, just shoot us a text. Even if it's an emoji, we'll be here."

I nod, and he leans across the counter, hand skating against mine as he kisses me goodbye. The kiss is the silent promise that he's just a text away.

Dax follows suit, leaning forward to give me a kiss too. I keep him a fraction of a second longer than necessary, a kiss that says he is utterly mine. I feel his hand find the nape of my neck, his grip gentle, but the way he kisses me is hard and possessing.

I catch Sav shooting us a death stare from the side.

Good! I think as I finally pull back, locking eyes with Dax before he backs off.

As they exit the bar, the door creaks. The place feels even emptier without them, even as the shenanigans continue at the pool tables.

EIGHT

DAX

The Christmas market is crowded. Above me, strings of lights twinkle, and it smells like roasted chestnuts and Glühwein. Lyka and I walk across the stalls, the cold nibbling at our cheeks but not hard enough to spoil the holiday spirit.

We have the beef Flora wanted, but Lyka is still on a mission. I see him, eyes darting across the stalls, running across all the handicrafts, trinkets, and gifts. He stops at a stall selling body lotions and candles and bends down to have a look.

While he inspects them, I glance over to the next stall, and the jewelry catches my attention. On display are dozens of pretty necklaces, bracelets, and rings. I zero in on one piece.

Beautiful. A deep green sapphire sits right in the center of the ring, flanked by diamonds on either side. It's simple but elegant.

"Hello, can I help you, sir?" a voice brings me back. A small woman stands behind the stall, bundled up in a scarf.

"Yes, please," I say while nodding toward the cabinet. "Mind if I take a look at that ring?"

Her gloved hands move quickly to open the cabinet, and she

pulls the ring out. As she raises it, the light refracts off the stones. *If it doesn't fit, I can get it resized.*

I take the ring and marvel at how beautiful it is. I can see it on Flora's finger. It would look amazing against her one green eye. The mere image shoots a pang through my chest. I glance over at Lyka, who's still engrossed in his shopping. I wasn't supposed to buy something this important today, but it feels right.

"I'll take it!" I exclaim.

She smiles and nods, naming the price. Yeah, it is expensive, but something this nice was never going to be cheap. I don't even bat an eye.

I don't care how much I just spent. It's for Flora, and honestly, she's worth every penny. The lady puts the ring in a little velvet box, wrapping it up nicely before she hands it to me.

"Enjoy," she says.

I can hardly hear her as I hold the box, flipping it open to take another look at the ring. Then, out of nowhere, Lyka chimes in.

"That better not be what I think it is…"

I look up as he approaches, instantly catching his narrowed eyes. I shut the lid fast; I don't want him to see too much.

He raises an eyebrow. "You aren't thinking of fucking proposing, are you?"

His question gets me off guard. *Propose?* It's the furthest thing from my mind, but the thought brings out deep emotions. *What if I really wanted to?*

I shake my head. "Nah, it's just a little bonus Christmas gift."

Lyka stares at me like he's trying to work something out. Then, he relaxes, arms falling to his sides.

"Oh, okay," he says with relief.

I ease the box into my back pocket, but one question keeps

popping into my head—what if? For now, though, it's just a gift —the best, most perfect gift for the woman I love.

LYKA

Dax approaches the food stalls, enticed by the smell of something on the grill. He has always been a sucker for market foods.

But I really can't focus on this anymore, my mind returning to that ring.

He said it was merely an extra Christmas present, but what if it is more than that? What if he is considering proposing? The thought eats at me.

It's not that I don't want Flora to be happy. Of course I do. Dax loves her, no doubt about it. But he has always been her first.

He was the man she had lost her virginity to. He heard those three words from her mouth first. *I love you.*

It shouldn't bother me. It's not as if we are competing. We share everything, even her. But it seems like he's always one step ahead. Now, with that ring in his pocket, what if he is the first to promise her forever?

I let out a sigh now, running a hand through my hair as I watch him order at the stall, oblivious to my thoughts. I know I should let it go—trust him and her—but the doubt lingers.

Dax swings around to face me, holding a corn dog with a big bite taken out of it.

"All set for tonight?" he asks with a mouthful. I can't help but snicker and shake my head.

"At least chew first and then ask me?" I joke, crossing my arms while leaning against the closest stall.

He swallows and leans in for another bite. "Seriously, we've got everything sorted, yeah? Food and decorations?"

"Yeah, yeah." I wave him off. "It's all sorted. The only wild-card is whether she's gonna have a good time."

Dax chuckles. "She really struggles with letting us do things to her, but can you blame her?" he says, continuing with another bite of the corn dog.

Fuck! My mind is still stuck on that damn ring in his pocket. Maybe I'm overthinking it.

The words come out before I can stop them. "You aren't planning something huge with that ring?"

Dax stops mid-chew, his eyes darting to mine. When he swallows, his face is unreadable. "I told you, it is a gift... Chill."

I peer at him a second and then shrug. "Okay. Just making sure..."

"Oh crap! The tinsel?" Dax asks suddenly, his eyes wide, like the thought just struck him.

I take the bag in my hand and let the thick strands spill out from the side.

"Don't worry, I got it."

A knowing smile stretches across his face as he finishes the last bite of his corn dog. "Sweet. I cannot wait for tonight."

I turn to Dax, and all he can do is stare back. Some things, only silence can say. Tonight isn't about Christmas. It is all about her, about making her feel special and loved.

And with the tinsel... *I can't fucking wait.*

NINE

FLORA

With every round of drinks, the group gets wilder. Laughter and screaming overwhelm the bar like a tornado. Sav clutches her beer bottle like it's a lifeline.

"Alright! Last call, everybody!" I yell, trying to sound unbothered. "After this, I am shutting things down!"

They dismiss me, paying more attention to the pool table. But Sav...she sways up to the bar, that bloody smirk stuck on her face as she sits on the stool. "What's it like, sharing them?" she mocks, leaning toward me with a grin. "Bet you feel lucky, like the only girl in the world."

I don't answer her. Turning around, I take a towel and wipe down the bar as if she isn't here.

But she keeps going. "Doesn't it bother you?" she presses. "Thinking about how they've been with most of the girls in this town? Including me."

I know about their past with women, but I know they are mad about me now, and that's all that matters.

I spin on my heel and glare at her. "You're just mad because he doesn't want you."

Sav's grin widens as she leans in even closer, nearly tumbling off the stool, she's so drunk.

"I could have Dax anytime I want," she says, slurring her words. "All I'd have to do is snap my fingers."

I can't help the laugh that bursts out of me.

"Really? Call him. You've got his number, right? Let's find out."

Before she can get another word out, I snatch the beer bottle from her grasp, my grip tight as I yank it free. "Just fuck off." I nod toward the door.

She takes a moment and glares at me, squinting like she's figuring me out. Then, she leans back.

"How is Dax?" she asks, falsely curious. "I completely understand how strange he gets this time of year…"

Her words make my chest tighten, but I keep a straight face.

Sav says with a sly smile, "Let me guess: he trusts you, huh? But I wonder if you know he killed his mom and dad." She stops for a second, as if letting it drop like a bomb. "He told me when he was hammered on New Year's Eve some years back."

My heart stops. Ice floods my veins.

"What do you fucking want?" I manage to utter.

She flings one quick glance back, but the guys are too interested in their drinks to take notice. Then, she points a finger in my direction, her nail almost touching my chest.

"Wouldn't it suck," she taunts, "if somebody messed up your little kinky three-way thing and ran to the cops to spill the beans?"

Sav's sinister laugh gives me goosebumps. When she hops off the stool, she sways, a bit wobbly as she strolls back to the gang.

She wouldn't actually do it, would she? It's Christmas… Nobody is calling the cops today or tomorrow. But if she actually does…

I will not let her screw this up—screw *us* up. Dax and Lyka mean everything to me. They're all I fucking have left. I can't stand losing them too.

The gang starts to head toward the door. Sav hangs back a little, flashing one last grin before following them.

The door closes behind her, and the fear I kept stored away bursts out. I rush over, fumbling with a shaking hand, and throw the lock shut with an audible click.

I scream. It's raw. Frustrated. Helpless. It bounces off the walls of the empty bar while tears stream down my face.

I take deep breaths to calm my nerves and tell myself one simple thing: no chance in hell Sav is going to blab to the cops tonight. She's too drunk. She's just getting sick pleasure from the threats she was throwing around. *How could she do that to him? He was an abused child! Hopefully, she will sober up and forget.*

I finish locking up the bar before I head out into the cold night. I shiver as I hurry to the truck.

The engine starts without a hitch. *Thank fuck.*

The heater whirrs to life, struggling to warm the truck. I want to call Dax and fill him in on what Sav said, but I don't. This isn't a conversation to have over the phone—it's too big, too important.

Kicking into gear, I pull out of the parking lot onto the snow-covered asphalt, tires crunching on the ice.

I know Dax and Lyka have something in store for me. I've seen the way they've been acting. However, I find myself unable to focus on the road. What if Sav doesn't forget? I grip the wheel harder, trying to force all those thoughts away, focusing on the drive to the cabin. As I continue down the curvy road, something is illuminated by my headlights. At first, it is difficult to see, but as I get closer, I realize it's Sav.

She stumbles as she makes her way up the side of the icy road. My stomach churns in disgust. *Great friends she has, letting her stumble home alone.*

But then, I remember what she said—how she's gonna tell the cops, how she's gonna screw it all up.

It twists my chest, the fear and the anger combining into something darker, uncontrollable. I will not let her screw with my family.

You will not fucking destroy us!

Anger surges through me; before I can think, my foot slams down on the gas, and the truck picks up speed. I hold the wheel tight. Sav cocks her head when she hears the truck.

She spins around, blinded by the strong headlights. She lifts a hand to block it.

The truck hits her with a sickening bang. She flips onto the hood and bounces off into the snow. I can't breathe. My hands are stuck to the wheel as the truck slows to a stop.

What have I done?

I throw the truck in park and jump out the door. I hurry over to her. All I can hear is the crunch of snow beneath my boots.

Sav is splayed out in the snow, nose bleeding, face pale. She blinks a few times. Her hand reaches out for me weakly.

I fall to my knees beside her, heart racing. The steam of my breath comes out in hard currents as I snarl, "You're not gonna break me. Got it? Dax is mine. He's my whole damn world!"

She grunts, mouthing something.

"You're an entitled little bitch who truly doesn't care what he went through! *He was a child!*" I spit, the acid in my voice surprising me.

I scan the darkness, confirming no one's here. I turn back to her. "You thought you won, huh? You're wrong. He did it for me, and I'll do it for him."

Sav's body twitches.

I leap up, dashing back to the truck. Shaking all over, I yank the door open and hop inside. The radio turns on, and "Left Outside Alone" by Anastacia blares. It's kind of funny how well it fits—poetic justice, you know? She's going to be left outside alone.

I glance in the rearview mirror, the glow of the tail lights illuminating her body in the snow. My jaw clenches, teeth straining.

I waste no time putting the truck in reverse and punching the gas. The truck jerks backward, and its tires roll over her body with a sickening pop, like crushing a watermelon.

I get out of the truck again to examine the mess I made. Her head—I hardly recognize it. I can't bear to look at it in detail. A mess of blood and bone smear together in the snow.

I kick her body with my boot, and she rolls into the ditch by the side of the road.

"Merry Christmas," I taunt.

I scan my surroundings again, finding an empty road surrounded by trees.

I jump back into the truck and slam the door shut, grasping the wheel tight as I work to catch my breath. My hands shake, but I know one thing for sure: Sav isn't gonna mess anything up.

The truck roars to life, and I drive off, leaving her body behind.

The song reaches its chorus, and Anastacia's voice blasts through the speakers, the perfect soundtrack to my mess. Before I know it, I'm singing along. My heart beats so loudly, it nearly drowns out the music for a second.

I have absolutely no idea what to do.

My head is all over the place, thoughts bumping into each other. *What if someone finds her? Nah, they won't until after Christmas. She's gonna be buried under more snow anyway. What if someone did see? Chill out, Flora.*

I shake my head, trying to break up the panic. Nobody saw anything. There's no one around. She's gone, and she can't hurt me, Dax, or Lyka. *My men.*

The rest of the drive is a blur as my head spins from a cocktail of adrenaline and fear. I just need to get to that cabin, to them. They will know what to do.

TEN

DAX

I SET THE MATTRESS IN THE MIDDLE OF THE BARN, MAKING SURE IT looks good. It smells pleasantly of wood mixed with just a hint of smoke from the log burner Lyka is tending. It has really started to warm up in here, and the fairy lights hanging from the rafters make the whole barn feel magical.

"You think she'll like it?" I ask.

Lyka looks over his shoulder, fiddling with the log burner.

"Hope so..."

I exhale a breath and nod to myself, taking it all in. The tinsel looks amazing hanging along the edges of the mattress. Each sex toy is ready, all decked out with festive vibes. The gingerbread houses Lyka whipped up sit on the little table beside the mattress, and I can't help but smirk. I know they contain something extra special. This is going to be one Christmas she will remember, that's for sure.

Lyka walks over with a beer in hand, takes a long swig, and looks at me.

"I got this weird feeling, like we should've grabbed her from the bar."

His words catch me for a second, and I turn to him.

"She'd call or text if something was up," I say, but I can't help the creeping sense of unease making its way up my spine. "If she doesn't show up in the next ten minutes, we'll take a drive. I just want her to feel free, ya know? Particularly after everything…"

Lyka nods, but I can see he isn't quite reassured. I try to distract him, grabbing the funny underwear we picked out earlier. I hold it up, and the silly reindeer face with a bright red nose makes me grin.

"She's gonna crack up when she sees these." I smile and wave the underwear in front of him.

Lyka shakes his head, a muffled laugh escaping him. He reaches out reluctantly to grab the underwear.

"I can't fucking believe you talked me into wearing this," he says, holding them up like some sort of cruel joke.

"Ay, her face is gonna be priceless," I say, grinning even bigger. "Come on, let's put them on."

I strip down, yanking my shirt over my head and slinging it across the pile of hay nearby. At least it's warm in here—Jesus, the last thing I need is some cold air causing my cock to shrink. I giggle at the thought as I shimmy out of my pants.

Lyka looks at me for some time before heaving a sigh and stripping down himself. He's not happy about it, but he's doing it for her.

Soon, we are both standing buck naked, instinctively covering our cocks.

I carefully slide into the underwear, pulling it up and adjusting so everything fits snuggly into that ridiculously over-sized reindeer face, the red nose right there in the middle. I look down, and it hits me how silly this all is.

I laugh when I check myself out. "Oh my God. This is so fucking ridiculous."

Lyka gives me a raised eyebrow—he's really trying to stay cool, but I can almost see the corners of his mouth twitch.

"You look like a demented Rudolph," he says.

"Oh, shut it. It's your turn," I say, still laughing as I motion for him to put his on.

Lyka grumbles but eventually slips into the underwear, defeated. When he finally looks at himself, he erupts into a fit of laughter.

Lyka turns around and reaches for something on the table, and *oh my God!*

His bare ass is on show. I've never taken notice before, but it's impressive. Firm.

He picks up the red baby doll set we got for Flora. The shiny satin glimmers in the fairy lights, and the white faux fur around the edges makes it festive, just the sort of thing a hot Mrs. Claus might wear.

"Damn," Lyka mutters. "Just thinking about her wearing this is getting me hard."

I look down and see his reindeer underwear stirring as his cock twitches against the cloth.

"I can totally tell, dude," I say, nodding towards the obvious evidence.

Lyka shoots me a look and shakes his head. "Oh, shut up!"

He takes his time folding the baby doll set back in its spot. It's pretty funny, looking at his reindeer-patterned bulge, but at the way his hands grip the fabric, he's just as pumped for tonight as I am.

"Can you blame me? She's gonna look totally perfect in this."

I nod, imagining her in it. "Abso-fucking-lutely."

Lyka knocks lightly on the wood.

"You know, putting up the tinsel earlier, I felt this really weird chill," he says, "like something wasn't right. I don't know."

I pause. Usually, Lyka's the cool, calm, collected one, so hearing him say this puts me on edge.

I reach into my pocket and pull out my phone.

"I'm gonna call her," I say, my thumb hovering over her name in my contacts.

But before I press call, the truck pulls up outside.

"Phew! Right on cue—she's back," I say, placing my phone on the table.

Lyka looks relieved as he takes a swig from his beer and nods toward the barn door.

ELEVEN

FLORA

I jump out of the truck, my hands shaking. My mind races so fast, I can hardly keep up with it. *How do I tell them?* Do *I tell them?*

Fuck. Panic and guilt whirl together inside my gut. *Do I wait till tomorrow?* I don't want to ruin whatever they have planned, but am I even capable of looking them in the eyes and acting like everything is cool?

"Fuck, fuck, fuck..." I mutter under my breath. The urge to slap some sense into myself is overwhelming, but I understand it won't help a bit.

I trudge up the path toward the cabin—it's dark, the windows black. For a moment, my heart sinks. *Where are they?*

Then, I see a light coming from the barn, Christmas music drifting up.

I freeze. My men are waiting for me. I can't ruin this for them.

I breathe in deeply. *One step at a time, Flora.*

I enter the barn, and fucking hell, is it a sight. It's right out of a Hallmark movie. Warm, twinkling fairy lights hang from just about everywhere, hanging from the beams. Then, there's a projector with snow coming down, sprinkling soft, sparkling flakes across the walls and ceiling. It's magical.

Wow, they've just gone all out.

Lyka and Dax stand next to each other in front of a mattress piled with throws and pillows. I first notice their matching smirks, and then my gaze wanders to what they're wearing.

I can't help it. I burst out laughing, holding my stomach as I bend over. They are so proud of themselves, and it's completely ridiculous. It's just what I need.

Then, it hits me.

My laughter dies as I remember what happened—the truck, the ditch, the crunch of bone, and suddenly, my laughter turns to tears.

"Flower?" Dax says, concerned. I rush to Lyka and leap into his embrace.

His strong arms wrap around me, and I press my face against his chest. The heat of his body is comforting, but it doesn't keep the tears at bay.

"Baby, what's up?" Lyka tries to calm me down.

I can't tell them, not now, not yet. I choke back a sob, holding him tightly as I force the words out. "Nothing," I manage, my voice shaking. "I'm just...so happy. You two are amazing. This is all so beautiful."

Lyka looks down at me, his brow scrunched, but he doesn't push me to say more. He rubs my back in slow circles while Dax moves closer, his hand pushing my hair out of my face. "You sure, Flower?" Dax's eyes search mine.

I nod, plastering on as good of a smile as I can give. "I'm just so overwhelmed. This... It's perfect."

They exchange a glance, but neither pushes the matter. Lyka presses a kiss to the top of my head while Dax places a quick one on my temple.

I hold onto them both, praying that, just for a little longer, I can hold off the weight of what I've done.

I lean back, rubbing my eyes and trying to focus on them. My eyes wander down to their goofy underwear. "You two look ridiculous."

Dax steps back, grinning mischievously. He begins swaying his hips from side to side, his cock is swinging under the fabric —it's just so fucking funny.

"Oh my God, stop it!" I exclaim, holding my stomach. "I am going to pee myself with all this laughing."

Lyka rolls his eyes at Dax as he ambles over to the little table by the log burner. He grabs something red and silky and holds it up for me to see. "Well, beautiful, we got you this."

It's thin, almost see-through. I feel my cheeks burn just staring at it.

"Gosh!" I exclaim, stroking the material. It's almost weightless.

Dax comes up behind me, his warm hands on my hips. "Let's get this on you, Flower."

In one, swift move, he pulls my shirt up and over my head before I can utter a word.

Lyka backs up to give Dax space as he continues to strip me. His hands are so confident, unleashing my bra and pulling the straps down my arms. I glance quickly over my shoulder at him, and my heart races with the look that passes between us.

"You're gonna look even more beautiful in this," Dax says, leaning down to plant a kiss on my shoulder while he takes the babydoll from Lyka.

Dax drapes the fabric down my body, and it sends a shiver through me. He steps back, eyeing me up and down. Then, Lyka joins in, crossing his arms, tilting his head a little.

They both stare at me, their eyes soaking in how the babydoll fits, how it hugs, how it shows everything off just perfectly.

In their eyes, I feel seen—really seen. They do not see just the outfit and the playful holiday setup. They see me. Admiration, want, and love are etched across their faces, clear and unfiltered.

"Wow, you're absolutely beautiful," Lyka breathes.

"More than beautiful," Dax says, his smile turning mischievous. "You're the only girl in the world, Flower."

They make me feel like I'm their whole world. I catch a glimpse of myself in a little mirror on the table, and I just can't help but feel sexy.

I run my hands over the fabric, and my lips curl into a playful smile.

"Do you like it?" I ask, but their faces give it away.

"Like it?" Lyka laughs and shakes his head. "We fucking love it."

Dax steps closer, swiping a piece of hair from my face as he bends down. "And we love you. We've got so much planned for tonight."

Lyka reaches out, sliding his hand into mine to pull me toward the mattress. My heart quickens as I lower myself, the mattress giving way under me.

Dax steps forward, holding a tray with a gingerbread house on it. The detailed design catches my eye—its little marshmallow decorations glint in the light, but something is off.

I lean in, taking a closer look. "The icing seems kinda weird..." I look up at Lyka. "You made this gingerbread house, didn't you?"

I know he's not the stronger baker between them.

They exchange knowing looks, as if sharing some private joke.

"What?" I ask, my brow furrowing.

He bends slightly at the knees, keeping the tray level.

"Flower," he starts off, "the icing is made from our—"

"Your what?" I jump in, looking at them.

Lyka leans in closer, his smirk spreading wide. "Cum."

I blink, my mouth falling open a little as I process his words. My cheeks flush hot before a disbelieving laugh bubbles out of me.

"You two are really something, you know that?"

Dax places the tray on the mattress beside me. "Wanna try a piece?" he asks, staring right at me, daring me, teasing me.

I bite my bottom lip. Their eyes are dark with anticipation. This is what they want. They want me to like it.

My hand hovers over the gingerbread house, my fingers just barely caressing one of the pretty edges. I break off a piece and hold it between my fingers.

Their focus is entirely on me as I bring the piece to my lips and slowly lick it. The saltiness of their cum melts on my tongue. *Fuck, I love tasting them.*

I can't help getting hot seeing their eyes light up in satisfaction.

"That's our fucking girl," Dax chokes out, his voice thick with approval.

Lyka's face is close to mine as he places his hand delicately on my knee with a grin.

"Knew you'd like it," he whispers, the tone playful but possessive.

With that, the entire atmosphere is charged.

"I think it's only fair you taste my cum on the gingerbread too," I tease.

They share a fast glance, like they're in some silent agreement. In a heartbeat, before I can even prepare, Dax shoves me back on the mattress, his hands on my shoulders. *His eyes, his fucking golden eyes. They make me weak.*

Lyka doesn't waste any time, sliding between my legs. His

hands run up my thighs, firmly clamping and spreading them wide open.

"Well, we are going to make you come first," Lyka whispers.

I want to say something, but before I can even get the words out, Dax leans in and kisses me. Lyka's fingers work up my inner thigh, and then he spreads me open. The air hits my wet core.

"Such a pretty pussy," Lyka breathes. His words send a rush through me, making my stomach knot in excitement.

Dax's tongue winds around mine, sliding into my mouth, making my toes curl. The kiss is needy as Lyka's finger finds my clit, starting off with slow, deliberate circles, teasing and testing, before he gives it just the right amount of pressure.

A moan releases within me, muffled against Dax's lips, as my body arches off the mattress. The feel of Lyka's expert touch blends with Dax's dominating kiss, sending stars reeling in my eyes, every nerve alive and screaming with pleasure.

"Good girl," Lyka says slowly, his finger continuing to work its magic.

I'm helpless, my body quivering as they push me further into the vortex of my longing.

Dax pulls back from my lips, his hot breath skating down my skin as he goes lower, his hands gliding along my sides.

"I'm just going to put my fingers here," he murmurs, looking at Lyka for approval.

I feel his fingers go to the sides of my clit in a V shape, framing it.

Lyka leans closer, and I hear him spit. The warm liquid lands on my pussy, and a little gasp escapes my mouth.

Without warning, Lyka's palm presses firmly against my clit. He rubs in small circles, and their touch is overwhelming in the best possible way—the combination of Dax's precise positioning along with the firm pressure of Lyka's making my clit swell against Dax's fingers.

I groan, letting my head fall back onto the mattress as the pleasure hits.

They coordinate flawlessly, their full attention on me.

"You're doing amazing, beautiful," Lyka says, moving faster.

"She's just so damn perfect like this," Dax adds, applying more pressure.

They move in sync, and the only thing I can do is surrender. My moans fill the barn as the fire crackles and the music plays in the background—it is pure.

I'm in fucking heaven.

Lyka's palm presses onto my clit, and I can feel the heat of his other hand, his fingers at my entrance. "She's so wet, Dax," Lyka says in a hushed tone, his finger pushing into my pussy.

Dax repositions his fingers, keeping the V shape as he wiggles them. The movements shoot jolts of pleasure through my already hypersensitive body.

"You feel that, Flower?" Dax says, his voice strong as he leans in. "Come for us."

The way their hands feel against me—it's just fucking right, the wild pressure surging inside me. It all hits me at once, and I can't hold it in any longer.

I cry out, the sound completely wild as the orgasm hits me. My body convulses, my thighs clamping down of their own accord as waves of pleasure crash over me.

"Oh my God!" I scream, my voice shaking as I arch my back off the mattress.

Lyka continues. His fingers fully slide into me, curling before darting around, as if he wants to collect every drop of my release.

Dax doesn't pull fingers back. He keeps my clit exposed, absorbing every little bit of pleasure.

I'm shaking, my breathing short and messy, aftershocks from my orgasm wreaking havoc on my body.

A low moan escapes my lips as Lyka's fingers slide out of me. I watch through half-lidded eyes as he grabs the gingerbread house and snaps a piece off.

He returns to me, on his knees between my legs again. I catch the delicious scent of gingerbread just before I feel Lyka push the piece against my slit.

The edges glide over my folds as he gathers every bit of my arousal. With the other hand, he keeps me open so I can't squirm away.

"Get every drop," Dax orders as he watches.

Lyka raises the gingerbread slightly, the piece glistening with my juices. Without a single second of hesitation, he presses it to his lips, his tongue darting out to lap up the flavors. His eyes shut for a second before a growl escapes his lips.

"Dude, she tastes amazing," he breathes.

Dax leans forward and snatches the gingerbread from Lyka's hand. Smirking, he flips it over in his fingers. The edges become a playground for his tongue as he scrapes off residual slick, his eyes meeting mine in a smug, satisfied gleam.

"I can still taste her on my tongue," Lyka says.

The moment Dax hears the confession, his eyes go dark. He moves closer to Lyka, his hand sliding to the back of his neck, his fingers grasping tight as he pulls him in.

"I wanna taste her on your tongue."

Their mouths slam together, lips parting instantly. Their tongues glide together, sharing me. Lyka groans low, his hand rising to grip Dax's shoulder as they deepen the kiss. Fuck, I can't look away.

I watch, mesmerized, as two powerful, commanding men

share a raw, passionate kiss. It stirs inside a new kind of longing.

They pull away and turn toward me. I feel a tingling sensation in my tummy, like a thousand butterflies. I release a series of embarrassing, nervous giggles upon seeing the smirking grin on Dax's face.

"Do you think she's on the naughty or nice list, Lyka?" Dax asks in a mocking tone.

Lyka crosses his arms, as if in deep thought. "Hmm, well, she has certainly given me attitude a few times."

Dax raises a brow, his lips threatening a smile as he inches closer. "Oh really? You've been naughty?"

"Maybe," I tease.

Lyka stands from the mattress and approaches the workbench. A few seconds later, he turns around with something familiar: the wooden paddle has been used on me before, but now, its handle is wrapped in silver tinsel.

"Just because it's all dolled up with tinsel doesn't make it festive," I say, attitude in my voice.

Lyka snorts, playing with the paddle as he advances. "See? There it is, her fucking attitude."

Dax picks a strand of tinsel off the mattress then drops to his knees before me. "Naughty girls get punished. Get on your knees and turn around."

I follow his command, shuffling onto my knees. I turn away from them, anticipation coursing through me.

"Hands behind your back," Dax orders.

I gulp hard as I obey. My heart races as the thick tinsel wraps around my wrists. He pulls the tinsel tight enough to hold my hands in place without hurting me. It feels so good, and I'm so ready for it.

"You're super obedient, huh, Flower?" Dax says softly.

Dax slaps his hand on my back, sending me into the

mattress. My face falls into it, and I can feel myself breathing harder.

Before I can even settle in, Lyka's firm hands grip my hips, pulling my ass into the air. I'm totally exposed, and yet I'm buzzing with excitement.

Dax's large hands wrap around my jaw, pulling my head upwards. His thumb strokes my cheek.

"I'm just gonna take these off," he says, shoving the silly reindeer underwear down and tossing them aside. His cock pops out, hard and veiny, the tip already glistening.

"Alright," Dax continues, inching closer. The head of his rosy cock presses against my lips. "While Lyka's doling out your punishment, you're gonna take my cock in that cute little mouth of yours, aren't you?"

He runs his finger along my bottom lip.

"Ye...yes," I stammer, the excitement shaking my very core.

Without warning, his hand fists my hair, his fingers tangled firmly in the strands as he pulls my head forward, pressing the tip past my lips. He slowly forces me to take more of him.

Then, I feel a hard smack across my ass as that wooden paddle bites into me. I gasp around Dax's cock.

"This'll get you back on the nice list," Lyka says, rubbing the paddle on my skin before giving another solid smack.

Dax groans over me, his hips shifting just enough for me to take him right to the back of my throat. My gag reflex kicks in for a second, but I focus on breathing through my nose.

"Oh, totally..." Dax says, sounding satisfied as he guides my head up and down on his cock. "That'll get her back on the nice list for sure."

Lyka lands another sharp spank with the paddle on my other cheek, and the sting blooms into a warmth spreading across my skin. "I'm leaving some really nice marks on her." He sounds proud of himself.

"Well, she's ours to mark," Dax says over me.

They just won't let up, their hands and words engulfing me. Saliva drips from the corners of my mouth as I work to take Dax in deeper. Every single time I bob my head, another groan leaves him, his cock twitching against my tongue.

Suddenly, the paddle slaps on the barn floor. I barely get a second to wrap my head around it before something soft but firm wraps around my throat. It's tinsel, and Lyka tugs on it.

I gasp around Dax's cock as the feeling sends a wave of heat down to my pussy, and my body responds instinctively.

I feel Lyka's cock right behind me, nudging at my entrance, his tip teasing. I catch my breath when he leans down, his chest sliding against my back while his lips go for my ear. "You want me inside you, baby?"

I try to say something, but Dax goes deeper, his cock totally filling me up, with no room for talking. Instead, a moan escapes me, vibrating around him—muffled yet full of need.

Lyka bursts out laughing, and the sound runs like electricity through my veins. The tinsel on my throat tightens as he jerks me back enough to make me arch.

He plunges his cock into me in one smooth motion. The combination of sensations—the fullness of Lyka inside me, Dax's steady rhythm in my mouth, the pull of tinsel on my throat—is too much.

"That's our girl," Lyka says, taking it slow.

"She takes us like a pro," Dax says, impressed.

I take them like a pro every time.

I'm sandwiched between them, consumed, with no place for thought—just pure, intoxicating pleasure.

Our bodies move in tandem. The barn fills with the sounds of our mutual desire, skin slapping, ragged breathing, muffled moans.

Lyka's thrusts slow down. "Fuck, we better slow down," he says, slightly strained. "If we wanna last…"

Dax gives a sharp tug on my hair, and my head angles back. His cock pops from my mouth, swollen and slick, and a line of drool dribbles down onto the mattress beneath.

I let out a sharp gasp, my chest rising and falling with the effort of catching my breath, but Dax doesn't give me a second to cool down. His hands tangle in my hair, holding me right where he wants me as he leans down to press his lips to mine.

He doesn't even care that my mouth's still wet with saliva. His tongue slips past my lips, taking me over as his taste mixes with mine. The whole mess just seems to make him want it more.

I moan into the kiss as he totally devours me. Behind me, Lyka's hands grip my hips, his slow thrusts stretching me out.

"You're ours, Flower," Dax whispers against my lips. "All fucking ours."

I will always be theirs. They have total control over me.

Lyka thrusts into me one last time, riding out those final waves of mind-blowing pleasure. A deep groan rips from his lips, and he pulls out slowly, caressing me quickly before he finally lets go.

I let myself flop down onto the mattress, my arms and legs like lead.

The room's quiet, save for the sound of our heavy breathing and the crackling of the log burner. I barely register when Dax unties the tinsel from my hands. He and Lyka lay down beside me, one on either side.

Dax's arm drapes over my waist as he plants a sweet kiss on my shoulder. "We're not done with you yet. You get a little break," he whispers.

Lyka's hand runs softly up and down my back, as if to soothe me. His fingers are incredibly light, drawing patterns on my skin that make my body tingle. He leans over and presses a kiss against the top of my head, his breathing still a little ragged.

We all lay in silence, a nice, cozy kind of quiet.

Dax rolls off the mattress, and of course, I have to stare—mostly at his cock, still hard and glistening under the barn lights. He doesn't seem to notice—or maybe he does, because there's a smirk on his lips as he heads over to the table.

He offers me a bottle of water, the cap already twisted off. "Here you go, Flower. Lubricate that delicate throat of yours." He shoots me a cheeky wink.

Lyka rubs his hand on my back, giving me goosebumps.

"Thanks." I take a swig from the bottle.

Lowering it, I wipe my mouth with my hand and find myself looking between the two of them. These guys, who used to be my captors—the ones behind my nightmares—are now my whole world.

They broke me, reshaped me, and somehow, amidst all the chaos, they became my everything.

Lyka's hand pauses for a moment against my skin, like he understands what's going on in my head. Dax is just lounging at the edge of the mattress, looking at me with this half-teasing, half-sweet grin.

No matter what has gone down between us , I wouldn't want it any other way.

Lyka props himself up beside me, his hands delicately framing my face. His thumb traces over my cheek, and there's an urgency there, like he needs something from me.

"Kiss me," I whisper.

He leans down and kisses me softly and slowly, never breaking the seal of our lips. He eases me back to the mattress as he continues his frantic exploration of my body.

His kisses drift down my neck. His hands slide over my sides as he goes lower, tugging at the Christmas babydoll. Finally, my breast is exposed.

When his lips reach my nipples, he stops for a second, swirling his tongue around one, his hand cupping the other. It sends shivers all over me as I lean into him, wanting more of his touch.

But Lyka doesn't stay there for long. His kisses continue, slowing even further when he reaches that small, raw reminder of what I survived—the "F" brand scarred across my lower stomach.

He pauses.

"I'm so fucking sorry, Flora." His voice is full of regret.

Before I can say anything, he leans in and presses a kiss to the mark. The heat of his lips to my scarred skin sends a wave of emotion rioting through me—forgiveness and understanding.

Dax joins us on the mattress. His fingers drift over the brand, as if he can just touch it away from existence. He gives me the same expression as Lyka—apologetic, respectful, and it does something to my chest.

There is no fear, no bad vibes, just an unsaid thing that what we have now is way stronger than all the pain we experienced.

Lyka clutches my wrist and motions for me to straddle his lap. My body moves instinctively at his silent command. I shift to sit on top of him, and my pussy rubs against the length of his cock, friction sparking a jolt of my pleasure.

He groans, hands on my hips to help steady me. His fingers dig deeper, reaching down to grab the base of his cock. The tip brushes against my clit, teasing me with just enough friction to make me shake. I catch my breath, every move almost overwhelming.

I moan, unable to hold back.

Lyka chuckles, positioning himself at my entrance. "You're gonna take all of it, baby."

I lower myself inch by inch, my thighs starting to shake as he stretches me bit by bit. Suddenly, his hands catch my waist, steadying me until I get accustomed to the size of him.

Even though I've had their cocks many times, I still can't get over their sizes.

"Does that feel good?" He leans in, pushing my hair to the side.

When I have taken all of him, I stop, enjoying the feeling of being so completely filled. I roll my hips, slowly at first, grinding against him. His lips wander along my neck, his teeth brushing against my skin as his hands help me move, pulling me in closer.

"Fuck, you're so tight," he whispers into my neck.

I quicken the pace, and my movements become more fluid. I can feel Dax's gaze on me as Lyka's teeth dig into my skin, the little bruises like promises.

Dax slides in behind me, and the mattress dips as he places his palm on my back, nudging me forward. My breasts squish against Lyka's bare chest, and his strong arms wrap around my waist, holding me tight. "Hold on to me, baby."

I hear Dax spit, and the wet sound has my heart speeding up as his fingers circle my ass. So soft, yet so promising. He's in no hurry, taking his time getting me ready, knowing what comes next.

By now, I have taken both plenty of times, but I still feel an excited buzz.

Dax spits again, and I can hear his fingers working his cock as he gets himself ready. I feel the tip of his cock poking at my asshole, teasing.

"Just relax," Lyka whispers in my ear, his thrusts slowing so I have a second to prepare.

Dax grips one of my ass cheeks, pulling it to the side as he angles for a better position. The stretch starts with the head of his cock pushing inside, the familiar burn makes me gasp. It's always tight, always intense.

I scream into Lyka's shoulder, the sound lost against his skin as I get used to Dax's cock. Lyka gives the top of my head a kiss, saying sweet things to lift me up while Dax keeps pushing, truly determined.

"You think her pussy's tight?" Dax growls. "Her ass is even tighter."

He presses on, the stretch burning until finally, I feel him completely inside me.

"Fuck... I'm in," Dax breathes, his hands holding my hips, pausing for a second, giving me time to adjust.

They're totally in sync, their bodies working together like magic. Lyka thrusts up into me, his cock hitting that sweet spot, while Dax pulls out and pushes back into my ass.

"She takes us so well," Dax mutters from the back.

Lyka cups my face to make me look up at him. "You're so perfect, baby."

I feel my body weaken, yet I don't want them to stop. It's building and building into a pleasure so real, nothing exists except them claiming me.

Dax's thrusts behind me hit faster, and he pushes deeper inside my ass with each stroke; meanwhile, Lyka starts slow.

Dax's hand becomes tangled in my hair, tugging hard enough that my head jerks back. His lips brush my ear, his breath hot and heavy. "I'm gonna fill you up with so much fucking cum, Flower."

He tugs harder on my hair, keeping me in one place while his hips crash into me.

I feel dizzy and lightheaded as Dax's teeth graze my earlobe. "Fuuuuck," he moans as he spills inside me.

Their moans are everywhere, and it hits me like a wave of desire. How could it not? The way they sound—completely enveloped in their own pleasure... *Fuck, it drives me crazy.*

Dax pulls out, and I am left gasping at the sudden emptiness. But before I get my bearings, Lyka's hands grab my waist and flip me over like I'm weightless.

His cock slips out of me, and for a second, I'm left empty and needy. Then, he pushes my knees to my head, my ankles locking. *Dominant.*

The thrill of it courses through me, and I'm ready for him again.

He aligns himself, his cock pressing against my wet entrance before he surges back inside me in one powerful motion.

Lyka goes to town, each move hitting my g-spot just right. I am soaked for him.

Dax moves next to him, his hand grazes Lyka's back before it slides up to his face. Their gazes lock before Dax leans in and kisses him hard.

It's intoxicating to see their mouths moving together, their tongues tangling as Lyka continues to fuck me.

"Lyka!" I yell, the word tumbling out with desperation. "Lyka...Lyka!"

Dax pulls back from Lyka's kiss to catch his breath. His dark eyes flash toward me for a fleeting second before he faces Lyka again. "Come. Fill her up, Lyka... I wanna see it ooze out of her."

Wasting no time, Lyka tightens his hold on my ankles, keeping me right where he wants me as he flexes. He quickens his thrusts, powering deeper with each one.

"That's it. Keep going. Fuck her harder," Dax commands, watching us intently.

I hear Lyka's cock pounding into me, my soaked pussy loud

as I take him. My body shakes under him. *He has never fucked me so hard before.*

I can't help but scream, and everything goes fuzzy.

Lyka's thrusts turn erratic, his hips moving faster, his hold on me tightening. He moans as he thrusts deep a final time, his cock twitching inside me as he comes. The feeling of him filling me sends another shiver through my shaking body, my walls clenching around him as he lets out a low, satisfied groan.

Dax is still on his knees as he reaches out and slaps Lyka's back, as if congratulating him.

Lyka drops down beside me, still shaking from the aftershocks.

Dax uses two fingers to pinch my lower lips together—still, the cum oozes out of me. He looks impressed.

The barn falls silent again, the stillness wrapping around us like a warm blanket as we come down from that crazed high together.

We sprawl across the mattress, tangled in hot flesh. We don't even bother searching for our clothes; we just enjoy the feeling of our sweaty, naked bodies intertwined. Of course, it's Dax who breaks the silence. "You think she's on the nice list now?"

Lyka's hand glides over my stomach.

"Oh, she's totally on the nice list now," he says, out of breath.

Their hands are on me everywhere, each touch a kind of exploration. It's like they have never touched a woman. Lyka's fingers glide over my hip, dipping along the curve of my stomach, while Dax's hand travels down my thigh, strong yet so gentle.

"So damn beautiful," Lyka says in a quiet voice, almost to himself, his hand traveling to the small of my back.

Dax leans in closer yet, and his lips brush against my temple as he tucks a stray lock of hair behind my ear. "You good, Flower?"

I giggle, sinking into the mattress. "I'm good," I say, my words slurring from exhaustion. "Just fucked...literally."

Their hands keep roaming my body, their touches like balm to my sore parts.

My eyelids get heavier with each passing second, and the heat from their bodies lures me into slumber. I am safe and so loved.

TWELVE

LYKA

With Flora, it's like every time is the first time. Seriously, I have no idea how many times we've done it, but it's never boring. The way her pussy tightens around me, how she lets go completely, drives me crazy every single time.

She's knocked out right now in my arms, relaxed and pressed up against me. Dax is beside her, one arm looped around her middle, spooning her like a shield. They look so calm, like nothing in the world can touch them.

I feel a weight in my chest as I realize how much I love them both. I could stay like this all night, just watching and holding them, soaking up the peace, though I'm hyped to see Flora's reaction when she wakes up to her Christmas presents tomorrow. Suddenly, she stirs in my arms.

First, it's just small movements. Her fingers twitch, she catches her breath. Then, it builds. She stiffens and begins to whimper.

"It's okay, baby. I'm here," I whisper, tugging her closer, hoping to soothe the nightmare.

Her cries wake Dax, and he quickly rubs his eyes as he sits up. "Is she okay?"

"Just a nightmare." I rub her back lightly.

And then, out of nowhere, Flora rockets upright, her scream slicing through the silence, beating her head with her fists. "I killed her! I killed her!"

Dax jumps in, grabbing one of her hands to hold her back while I take the other. "Hey, Flower. You're okay. It's just a nightmare."

There's a nanosecond before her eyes fly open when pure panic stares back at us. Tears stream down her cheeks, guilt and fear etched into her features. "I killed her." The words crack as they come out of her mouth.

Dax and I exchange a confused, concerned glance.

"Killed who?" I ask.

Flora takes a deep breath, hugging Dax tight while fresh sobs wreak havoc on her body. "I'm so sorry," she gets out. "I had to. I just had to."

Dax gives her back a rub. "Had to do what?"

She pulls back, her face scrunched up. "I killed...I killed Sav."

The room falls into stunned silence.

"Really?" Dax asks, eyes wide. He keeps her at arm's length and searches for a hint on her face that she doesn't really mean it.

"I killed her, Dax. I hit her with the truck...then I ran over her again."

My stomach drops.

"She said she knew what you did to your parents. She said you spilled it all that one night you were drunk. She was jealous, pushing my buttons, and said she was gonna go to the cops."

"Oh my God," I whisper.

Dax pulls Flora close, wrapping his arms tightly around her as she bursts into tears.

"I'm so sorry! I'm so, so sorry! I had to! She would have ruined everything!"

Dax looks surprised, but there's something darker in his eyes. His hands shake a little as he holds her, but he moves with purpose.

Dax reaches out and grasps Flora's chin, turning her face toward him. "Flora, where's her body?"

Flora? He never calls her that.

She shakes her head, refusing to give us an answer at first, tears running down her face. She turns away, but Dax tightens his grip, and I can tell by the narrowing of his eyes he is dead serious.

"Flora!" I call out, my voice edged with panic.

She startles at my tone and finally gets the words out. "Off Redwood Street...down in the ditch."

Dax and I look at each other, and it clicks. We know what we have to do.

Without a word, we jump up and scramble for our clothes, focused on what we must do next.

Dax yanks his jeans up, jaw set with determination.

Flora shuffles to the edge of the mattress. "I'm sorry."

Dax stops for a second, looking at her with unexpected gentleness. "Stop saying sorry, Flower. You did what you needed to do. Lyka and I will sort it out."

He tries to comfort her, but I can see how the heaviness of it all is weighing on her.

I kneel beside her, holding her face with one hand. "You stay here, okay? We've got this."

She nods weakly, wraps her arms around herself, and curls up into a ball on the mattress.

Dax shrugs on his jacket and looks at me. "Let's roll."

Fuck! He means business.

What's done is done, and there is no turning back. We'll do whatever it takes to keep her safe.

THE TRUCK RUMBLES DOWN THE DARK LANE, THE ONLY SOUND THE SOFT whistle of the wind streaming through the window. I take a big puff from my cigarette, feeling the smoke swirl in my chest before I blow it out.

We've both killed before, but this is different. Now, it's not just our hands stained with blood, but Flora's too. *She did this for us.*

The silence in the cab hangs thick until Dax finally speaks up. "When she tells us she loves us, do you think she actually means it?"

I turn to him, completely gob smacked, and hand him the cigarette.

"Are you serious right now, dude? Flora killed for you, and you're questioning whether she loves you?"

He takes the cigarette, inhaling deep. "I mean, we put her through so much. I feel like she has too..."

I slap the dashboard hard. "Don't you dare go fucking second-guessing her," I snap. "She made a choice, Dax. For you... For us."

He flicks the ash of his cigarette out the window, staring at the empty road. "I just... I don't want to lose her."

"We won't. We just can't fuck this up again." Dax nods, his hands tightening on the wheel as he takes another drag. I glance over again at him, softening my tone. "Let's get this sorted and then enjoy Christmas, okay?"

He says nothing and hands the cigarette back.

The closer we get, the narrower the road becomes. Shadows dance between the trees and the headlights.

"Okay, we're on Redwood," Dax says.

We comb the side roads, searching for evidence, and it's not long before we see faint tire tracks in the snow.

"Yo, up ahead." I point to the tracks.

Dax swings the truck over and pulls to a stop. We sit for a moment in the quiet cab before exchanging a look. We don't have to speak; we know what we have to do.

We jump out of the truck, and the wind rises slightly, carrying with it the scent of pine and something sharper, coppery—blood.

Dax is first to the ditch. He squats low, peering into the dark. "Goddamn, Flora, you really messed her up. Can barely tell who it is."

I move in closer, my boots crunching in the newly fallen snow as I lean forward to have a look. The body, crumpled and twisted, lies face down. Her arms are awkwardly splayed, and the blood around her head is frozen into the snow.

"Crap," I mutter, pulling myself together. I head back to the truck and lift the tailgate, grabbing one of the shovels. I whistle to get Dax's attention and toss him the other.

"Alright, it's go time," I say, slinging the shovel over my shoulder.

Dax makes his way over to the body, and I follow.

THIRTEEN

FLORA

I jolt awake, sitting up so fast, my head spins for a second. My heart pounds while I look around, confused. I'm in the cabin, lying on the couch. *Wait, I'm not in the barn.*

The fire crackles warmly. The cabin looks totally magical. There's just something about it that feels different, more alive, like the spirit of Christmas is all over the place.

I look around, noticing garlands I don't remember setting out, twinkling fairy lights outlining the windows, even more on the mantle.

Did they add more decorations while I was asleep?

Lyka squats by the Christmas tree, placing presents under it. His back faces me—he hasn't yet realized I'm awake.

Dax enters from the kitchen with a steaming cup in his hand before I say a word. His smile is wide, real, as he approaches me.

"Merry Christmas, Flower."

Lyka spins around, his face lighting up when he sees me. He sits down beside me, radiating with so much happiness, the corners of my lips can't resist quaking a little.

Dax hands me the mug, and I look down to find it's hot

chocolate piled high, with a big dollop of cream sprinkled with chocolate shavings.

But then I remember last night. "Wait! What about—"

Before I can get the words out, Lyka sets a firm hand on my leg, the touch reassuring. He shakes his head slightly.

"It's all been sorted. We're not gonna let it ruin our Christmas, and we're never gonna speak about it again, okay?"

I swallow hard, clinging to the words.

Dax chills on the armrest beside me, his hand grazing my shoulder while he looks down. "You're safe. We're all safe."

I take a sip of the steaming hot chocolate. Sweet and creamy, it warms me from the inside out. I lean back into the couch for a moment, thinking maybe everything really will be alright.

"I wanna kick things off with your gifts," I say.

"Wait, what about breakfast?" Dax asks, peering over the rim of his mug.

I wave my hand dismissively, already moving toward the Christmas tree. "That can wait. I wanna see you open your presents!"

Dax sets down his mug. "If that makes you happy, Flower," he says, walking over with me.

I drop to my knees in front of the tree and dig through the presents tucked under the branches. The excitement builds until finally, there it is: a flat package wrapped in forest green paper.

"Here it is!" I say, spinning around with the gift in my hand.

Dax and Lyka sit on the floor, stretching out their legs. I scoot back to them, the paper crinkling as I set the gift on Dax's lap.

He looks at it curiously, his fingers tracing the neat little folds. "What's this, Flower?"

I sit back on my heels to watch. "You'll see..."

Lyka snatches the remote and switches on the TV. It lands on a music channel playing Christmas tunes. The catchy songs fill the space, and I just hope they don't hit us with John Lennon's *Happy Xmas*.

Slowly, Dax tugs at the edge of the wrapping paper—drawing it out just to tease me.

When he finally rips off the last bit of wrapping, his face contorts, eyes widening.

"Oh, wow!" he exclaims, "It's a picture of me riding a bike. Wait a minute! No, it's a painting!"

He peers at the details, tilting the frame a little so the light hits the rich colors and fine strokes. He holds it out for Lyka to see. "Wow, this must've taken you ages..." Dax takes a deep breath. "It looks like a real photo. It's beautiful. Thank you, Flower."

He shuffles toward me and kisses me. My heart swells, and I can't help but grin as I watch him look over the painting again.

He likes it.

"Your turn, Lyka." I head back to the tree to find his gift.

I see the heavy box stuck under the branches, wrapped up in red paper and tied with a gold ribbon. Giving it a few tugs, I yank it out at last, planting it in front of him.

Lyka raises an eyebrow. He unwraps his gift, his strong hands getting through the paper until the wooden box underneath shows. The wood is smooth and polished, with a shiny brass latch right in the middle.

Lyka's eyes widen as he flicks the catch, opening the box to reveal a set of new woodcarving tools all laid out and ready to go inside. The shiny steel blades glint in the light at the end of each polished handle, with the Faulkner brand stamped on them.

"Baby! No fucking way!" Lyka shouts, staring at the tools as if they're the greatest treasure. "This must have cost you a lot!"

I shrug, grinning as his excitement brightens the room.

"Hey, your tools were pretty rusty and worn out. You needed some new ones," I reply as I watch him pick up one of the chisels and examine it closely.

"These are amazing. You really didn't have to do this."

"I wanted to! You're always making something, and you deserve the best tools available."

He places the chisel back in its place then pulls me onto his lap. "You're the best, you know that?" he says softly, his lips against my forehead.

Dax proudly holds up his painting again. "You've totally spoilt us."

I lay my head on Lyka's chest, soaking in all the happiness. This is just what I wanted for Christmas morning—something packed with love and totally memorable.

FOURTEEN

LYKA

I really can't believe Flora got me new tools. The way she thought it all out...it just astounds me. She really does know how much my craft means to me, how each piece I carve is not just wood, but part of my soul. She's something else.

We don't deserve her, but I'll spend the rest of my life trying to become someone who does.

Dax chills next to Flora, watching her eyes glitter as she unwraps the last of the smaller presents he got her.

I can see it in Dax's face, though. *It's time.*

"Right..." Dax's voice is different as he digs into his back pocket.

I freeze, watching him pull out the little velvet box. For a second, I think he's going to get down on his knee, and I'm gonna hit him. *Don't fucking do it, Dax.*

He squirms a little, but he stays seated. He coughs, clearing his throat before he extends the box toward Flora.

Her brow furrows in interest as her hand stretches to take it. She opens it gingerly, gasping when she sees the ring nestled inside.

"Dax! It's stunning."

Her fingers dangle there for a second, like she's terrified to touch something so fragile.

"It's sapphire. It made me think of you: strong, rare, gorgeous," Dax explains, blushing. *Okay, that's kind of cute. I've never seen him blush.*

I relax when he doesn't propose. My hands unclench, and I finally exhale.

Flora takes the ring from the box and slides it onto her finger. It fits her perfectly, like it was made for her.

The sapphire glows a deep, rich green as she raises her hand. It's both inconspicuous and beautiful, matching her own elegance perfectly.

Fuck, I can just picture a wedding ring on her finger.

Dax's smile grows wider, and his chest puffs out with pride as he leans back, pleased with her reaction.

The ring fits so well—man, Dax nailed it.

"Looks like it was made for you," I say, leaning in to check it out better. After a moment's pause, I take her hand. "I've gotta show you my gift now." I stand, pulling her with me.

"Wait, I got tons of gifts," she says, her fingers slipping between mine, as if trying to hold back.

"Trust me, you're gonna want to see this."

Dax stands too, nudging her behind with a playful smirk. "You're gonna love it, Flower."

I guide her along the hall, the floorboards creaking as we approach the room. "All right, close your eyes, baby."

She hesitates. "Lyka..." she starts, but she obeys.

I open the door and usher her into the room. "Now open, beautiful."

Her eyes flip open, and for a second, she's frozen. Her hands shoot to her mouth, eyes wide.

"Wait, no freaking way! You didn't!" she squeals, pivoting to take it all in.

The room is completely different. The walls are now lined with shelves loaded with paints, brushes, and canvases. In the middle of the room stand several easels I carved by hand with some fancy flower designs. Even the desk is hand-carved, flowers dotting the wood of the drawers.

"It's just amazing." The slight hitch in her voice betrays her emotions. Her hand skims the back of a chair, fingers tracing the etchings.

She twists back to me, her face going soft. "Hold on, this was your parents' room?" She looks between me and Dax.

I nod, catching Dax's eye, who crosses his arms and leans back into the doorframe like it's no big deal.

"Yeah, it was," I say. "But it was just sitting around. It was about time we put it to good use."

She turns back to me, her eyes shining with tears. Her lips quiver as she throws herself into my arms. She almost sends me stumbling, but I manage to keep her steady. "Everything's just perfect. This Christmas has been amazing. Thank you!" Her words come in like a wave, and I hug her closer.

"You're worth it, baby."

It's the least we could do, considering everything we did to her.

Behind her, Dax says nothing. He merely nods his head in approval as his eyes scan the room. For once, it feels like we've done something right—something just for her, to make her happy.

Suddenly, we hear a truck pull up outside. The rumble makes Flora startle, and Dax claps his hands together.

"Your Christmas is about to get even better, Flower."

Flora frowns. "What is it?" She edges forward towards the door.

I catch her wrist and drag her back before she can investigate.

Dax bursts out of the room, looking back and yelling as he heads out, "Keep her in there till I shout!"

"What's going on, Lyka?"

I place my hand on her shoulder. "Nothing bad, I promise."

We hear high-pitched yip emanating from the living room, and Flora whips her head toward the door. "What was that?"

Her face will be priceless when she sees her last gift.

I let out an extremely loud cough, trying hard to cover it and utterly failing. "What was what, baby?"

But before she can proceed, Dax yells out, "Alright, come in!"

Flora doesn't hold back. She breaks free from my grasp and races to the living room.

Dax stands there with something small in his arms. As we get closer, I make out the tiny, squirming figure of a Golden Retriever puppy, its floppy ears bouncing as it lets out another excited yip.

"And your final gift," Dax says, holding the puppy out to Flora.

She clasps her hands over her mouth, and her eyes well with tears. "Oh my God!"

She opens her arms, and Dax carefully lays the puppy in them. It squirms, straining to lick her cheek as she cuddles it to her chest.

"It's a girl," Dax says, strapping a dark pink collar on the puppy.

"She's a little angel, just look at her."

"Maybe that should be her name," I say.

Dax raises an eyebrow and looks at me, confused. "What, Little?"

And I call this man my brother.

I bring my hand to my face. "No, you idiot. Angel."

Flora giggles and raises the puppy so they're face to face. She peers right into her little eyes. "That's perfect. Angel it is."

Flora takes a sniff of the puppy's head. *Oh lord, here she goes again, sniffing things.*

"Puppies have a certain smell," she says with a shrug.

The puppy yips happily, her little tail wagging so fast, it's a blur as her sharp teeth nip along Flora's fingers.

Watching her, I just can't help but smile. The look on her face, the way she snuggles Angel—it's all I've ever wanted.

Flora looks up at me, her eyes sparkling. "This is the best Christmas I've ever had. I love you two."

I love you too, Flora.

FIFTEEN

FLORA

Seriously, this has to be the best Christmas ever. Never have I felt so spoiled, so completely overwhelmed with love. The ring on my finger, my gorgeous art room, and now little Angel all snuggled up and snoozing by the fire...

For the first time in a long time, I just feel... lucky.

But soon, the doubts begin to creep in. Could I truly be so lucky? I think of all I've endured with Dax and Lyka—how they broke me. But here I stand. I've seen how committed they are, felt it in ways most people could never fathom. They've killed for me, and I've killed for them.

As my thoughts begin to spiral, Lyka stands from the couch in a stretch.

"I'm gonna get a few more logs for the fire."

I glance over at Angel. She's asleep, exhausted from running in circles around the cabin.

From the TV, the opening notes of *The Power of Love* by Frankie Goes to Hollywood fill the room, soft but moving.

Dax stands from his chair and holds an arm out toward me.

"My lady," he says, a flirty smile on his face. "Care for a Christmas dance?"

Dax can dance? Oh, this will be interesting.

I reach for his hand and let him pull me up, his grip steady as he draws me closer.

He places one hand on my waist, lacing our fingers together with the other as we sway to the music. He leans in to croon the lyrics in my ear. *"I'll protect you from the hooded claw, keep the vampires from your door."*

I laugh as my voice harmonizes with the music as he whirls me around. When I finally face him again, his smile is pure mischief. "You're full of surprises, Dax," I say quietly, allowing him to lead this time.

"I am so in love with you," he sings.

Everything outside the cabin disappears—it's just us, the music, and the embers in the fire.

Then, Dax's voice goes quiet, serious. "I'm so sorry for everything we ever did to you, Flower."

I look up at him, and our eyes meet.

I should hate him. I should hate them both. But I don't.

He spins me around a final time, pulling me close, my back to his chest now. I bring my hand up, catching sight of the bright sapphire ring.

"The ring is beautiful, Dax. Thank you."

Dax points to my ring finger. "What if, someday, it's on that finger?"

It takes a moment for his words to sink in, and when they finally do, I wheel around immediately, trying desperately to read his face.

Marriage?

My mind wanders. An image forms—one that fills me with warmth and the feeling of surety I didn't know I was looking for.

Would I even have the strength to make it in this life without him?

Before I can speak, he smiles. "I love you, Flower."

"I love you too, Dax."

His lips find mine in an emotional kiss, the music playing in the background while we lose ourselves in the moment.

A very deliberate cough cuts through the silence. Lyka leans on the doorframe, grinning slightly as he takes in the view.

Dax, still holding me tight, gives me a sheepish grin and takes a step back, releasing me.

"I should probably get started on the food," he says, sounding super stoked to get cooking.

A little bark gets our attention as Dax heads toward the kitchen. Fully awake now, Angel bounces at our feet, her paws pattering hard as she nips playfully at our ankles.

"Alright, alright, little hellion," Lyka says, reaching to scoop her up, her tail wagging with furious abandon.

"The attitude of this little puppy," Lyka says, flashing me a teasing stare. "Totally like you, Flora."

I do not have an attitude.

I respond with a dramatic eye roll, flashing him the bird for good measure. "And yet, you totally adore me."

Lyka laughs, tugging Angel closer as she struggles in his embrace. "Yeah, yeah, just keep telling yourself that."

I GAZE AT THE CABIN, AND IT FEELS LIKE I AM IN ONE OF THOSE Hallmark movies. The green wreath hangs on the door perfectly, the bright red bow popping against the snowy background. Smoke snakes from the chimney, curling into the air. It all just feels so right, as though finally, things are balanced.

I step back, brush the snow off my gloves, and admire it all.

"Voila!" I exclaim, feeling proud. I lean my head and look at what I made.

Lyka stands a few steps to the side, shaking his head. "You do know it's normal to make a snowman, right? That's a snow bear."

"Ah, come on," I say, pulling the scarf off my neck and wrapping it around the bear.

Lyka crosses his arms. "Hey, don't blame me if you peek out the window later and see actual bears humping it."

How can he not like my bear? There's nothing wrong with it! *It looks fabulous.*

Before Lyka can say anything else, I grab a bunch of snow, form it into a ball, and throw it at his shoulder.

It hits him just right. Lyka freezes for a second, surprised.

"Oh, you're gonna pay for that, missy!"

I burst out laughing and take off running, boots crunching in the snow. His footsteps pound behind me, and I hear a snowball fly past my ear, barely missing me. "Missed me!"

But it's short-lived. His arm clamps around my middle, and in a whoop of laughter, we go tumbling down into the snow. Soft powder cushions our fall, and we laugh with Angel, who is obviously enjoying the mayhem as she barks and races around us.

We lay in the snow, panting, staring up at the gray winter sky as snowflakes start to fall, hitting my cheeks and eyelashes.

Lyka reaches for my gloved hand, and his thumb caresses my knuckles. "Hope you've enjoyed Christmas."

"I've absolutely loved it!" I exclaim. "You've spoilt me."

He says nothing for a while, continuing to stare at the falling snow.

"Maybe it's because we feel guilty about what we did to you," he finally says.

I sit up, shaking the snow off my jacket before I turn to him. He mirrors my movement.

"Hey, what happened in the past is just that—the past, Lyka. What really counts is the here and now. You and Dax...you guys have given me so much love and care. I'm lost in you. I'm tired of carrying that burden. I don't want to anymore, and neither should you."

He looks at me for a second, his eyes boring into mine.

"Here and now," he repeats.

I grasp his hand tightly.

Whatever darkness we've been through, whatever pain we've endured, feels like a distant echo compared to this moment. I just can't think of myself being anywhere else. The Cedarwood Cabin is more than a place—it's home. I want to stay here forever with Dax and Lyka in this life we've built together.

I'm lost in them.

Comfortable silence exists between us, but then, Lyka breaks it.

"Flora, I really love you."

He looks deeply into my eyes, and the way he whispers those words makes me feel weak every time. *Oh Lord, help me.*

His intensity tightens my chest. "I love you too, Lyka."

A small smile curls his lips before he turns serious. "Let's make you an official Faulkner."

I blink, utterly surprised. "What?"

Lyka grips my face between his hands, his gloved fingers barely touching my skin as he holds me. "Flora..." His voice trails off, like he's afraid to spoil this perfect scene. "Will you marry me?"

The words crash into me, and I choke up as my eyes dart to the cabin. Through the frosty kitchen window, I see Dax moving about near the stove, engulfed in whatever he's making.

I turn back to Lyka, and my mouth opens, but nothing comes out. He's not just asking me to stay, to keep living the life we've made together. He's asking me to be his, totally and completely.

DAX

I stop for a moment to gaze out the kitchen window, and what I see outside catches my attention. Flora straddles Lyka, her smile huge and free. Their foreheads touch like they are having a moment, Angel zipping circles around them in the snow, paws kicking up tiny flurries.

The image warms something deep inside me.

My family.

I take a moment to savor it as I lean against the counter. This is my life now—*our* life. It's insane to think we've actually made it this far.

I allowed the demons of the past to pull me into darkness, and Lyka, eaten by his guilt, followed along. We were broken, angry, and lost. Now, though, as I look at them, at this happiness we have carved out here, it's a new chapter.

I grab the knife again, the kitchen warm, the TV playing Christmas jingles.

And then, it happens: that damn fucking song kicks in. *Happy Xmas (War Is Over) - John Lennon.*

My shoulders tense, my grip on the knife tightening. That song—the one that raises all I've sought to bury. Those opening notes boil my blood as I step toward the remote, ready to turn it off and shut the noise out, but I hesitate. Instead of shutting it out, I stand and listen, actually listen, and let the words hit me this time.

"War is over if you want it…"

I just stand there for a second as the song plays. My chest is tight, but not from anger. It's something lighter.

Picking up the knife again, I start to chop the veggies as the lyrics fill my ears.

"War is over."

I look out of the window again to find Lyka and Flora still there, wrapped around each other in a kiss. *So full of love.*

I catch myself humming along, and my voice comes out soft yet steady. *"War is over..."*

Indeed, it is.

The war in my head, the storm brewing for so long—it's over. I inhale deeply as the tension in my chest releases.

All that matters now is what we have.

Our girl.

Our flower.

ACKNOWLEDGMENTS

Readers

I appreciate you dedicating your time to reading my book.
Thank you for everything.
In half a year you changed my life and I will never forget that.
I will miss each and every one of you.
All my love and goodbye.

Disturbed Valkyrie Designs

Girl! I don't even know what to say at this point.
Honestly, thank you.

Nadine

Thank you for being my alpha reader and helping me.

Daisy & Rachel

I love you.

Callum

"Why didn't ya put me in the acknowledgments? I play games
with you."
Thanks for putting up with me dude.

GET IN CONTACT

Email: jadewauthor@gmail.com

www.ingramcontent.com/pod-product-compliance
Lightning Source LLC
Chambersburg PA
CBHW031306120726
47906CB00003B/918